.

PRINTED IN THE UNITED STATES OF AMERICA
ON ACID-FREE PAPER
BY HADDON CRAFTSMEN, BLOOMSBURG, PENNSYLVANIA

ROCK SOLID

•

CHERYL COOKE HARRINGTON
&
ANNE NORMAN

,186

AVALON BOOKS
THOMAS BOUREGY AND COMPANY, INC.
401 LAFAYETTE STREET
NEW YORK, NEW YORK 10003

ROCK SOLID

To The Time Master
with love and appreciation

and

To Dr. Stuart Connolly
with gratitude

Chapter One

A billow of powdery grit rose around Rachel's feet to hang suspended in the sultry summer air. Far too warm for early June. And she was hot enough under the collar already. Her hands shook as she released the padlock, letting the heavy chain fall onto the sun-baked gravel road.

The arrogance. The unbelievable arrogance of the man. Riding the Wellman reputation into town, ready to take over. How dare he fence us out!

In her mind's eye, she pictured the smug faces of the partners at Bristol Foxworth O'Donnell & Kline. It was their scheming that had brought Street Wellman to town in the first place. Him and all his grand plans. Now, if they had their way, sleepy little Riverdale would become a bustling tourist mecca. And she was expected to help make it happen.

Rachel stormed back to her trusty red Jeep. Her strawberry blond hair, tied in a ponytail against the summer heat, bobbed in perky rhythm with every step, as if mocking the turmoil she felt. She gunned the engine, spinning the wheels and filling the air with dust, then raced across the

1

barrier as if the very act might destroy the thing. Wishful thinking.

The wheels locked as she screeched to a halt at the foot of the winding quarry road. *"Be sure you keep the entrance chained,"* they'd warned, and she stalked back to the gate, ready to do their bidding. *But no,* she decided. If someone wanted to go for a swim this afternoon, let them. Wellman Enterprises be darned. There may never have been the papers to prove it, but in hearts and minds at least, the quarry had always belonged to the people of Riverdale.

Leaving the chain where it lay, Rachel bent to retrieve the key. It had disappeared in the loose gravel, thanks to her fit of temper, and now she'd have to grub around in the dirt to find it. Peter would have laughed at her self-inflicted predicament. He'd always said that temper got her nowhere. She pushed his memory from her mind and redoubled her efforts to find the key, ruefully kicking at the gravel, finally catching the gleam of metal under the toe of her boot. It felt hot, she thought as she shoved it deep into her pocket. But it was only the sun's heat, not the devil's touch of Mr. Street Wellman. Sighing, she trudged back to the car. Like it or not, it was time to get to work. "I can do this." She said it aloud, to make herself believe. "I *can* do this."

The air felt cooler, smelled fresher, as she followed the old road down to Quarry Lake, and she felt herself beginning to relax. The place always had that effect on her, and she promised herself a swim before the day was out. Just the thing to calm her frazzled nerves.

One lone tree remained in the yard where the quarry plant and offices had once stood, and she claimed the patch of shade beneath it for the Jeep, fastening her key ring securely to her belt before she stepped from the car. It was a long walk back to town and she had no intention of making the hike.

Starting up the steep, wooded hillside, she wondered if

the cutoff jeans she'd chosen to wear had been a mistake. That tangle of underbrush, not to mention the bloodthirsty mob of mosquitoes that lurked within, would not be kind to her bare legs. She'd thought twice about it anyway. What if she met someone from the office?

She sighed. Except for Dotty, the firm's lovable but flaky receptionist, Rachel was the only woman in an office full of men. Most days it felt like every card in the deck was stacked against her, but Rachel Jennings-Porter was no "dumb blonde." She was determined to make them take her seriously, and clothes, it seemed, were an important part of the game. Not that there was anything wrong with her outfit, a pale blue tank top, modestly covered by a white, man-tailored shirt, tied at the waist. Nothing wrong with wool socks and work boots, either. The outfit suited the task. And, mosquitoes or not, it was too darned hot for long pants anyway, she thought, turning to rummage through the rolls of drawings that seemed to have taken up permanent residence in the backseat of her vehicle.

The Wellman survey had to be there. It *had* to be. She remembered throwing it through the window last night after her less than pleasant confrontation with Leon Bristol. He had laid down the law about exactly what her position was in the company; about how important Wellman Enterprises was for all of them; about how, if she wanted to keep her job, she'd better get with the program. "Okay," she said with a sigh, shaking her head to chase away the ghost of Leon, "the survey had a red elastic band around it . . . aha!" Thrusting the roll of drawings under her arm, she grabbed her notepad and camera and headed determinedly up the hill.

It was cool in the forest. A sharp and delightful contrast to the sun-baked quarry floor, and she lingered a while in the shade of an old white pine, watching an osprey wheeling lazy circles in the cloudless afternoon sky. She wondered if Barry Tarr knew about the osprey. Probably. Barry had told her all about the natural wonders on this site, as if she hadn't been coming here all her life. He'd been passionately adamant about the need to save the quarry's fragile ecosystem, as if she didn't know that everything could be wiped out in one fell swoop. And Barry had warned her, his voice deadly serious, that working on Wellman's team meant selling her soul, as if she hadn't been ready to quit her job rather than take on this project. But then who'd look out for the quarry? She had to stay, try to make it work. Maybe she could make a real difference—protect and enhance, not destroy.

Barry and his band of R.A.T.S. were ready to do their best to quash Wellman's marina project before the plans were even off the drawing board. And, before her unwilling recruitment to Wellman's team, she'd been tempted to join forces with Residents Against Turtle Slaughter. Knowing how devoted they were to the cause, and how fanatical they could be, she wondered if she was crazy to think they'd settle for a compromise.

Enough daydreaming. There was work to be done. She'd accomplished quite a bit already, as evidenced by the red pencil marks and jottings that had sprouted on the drawings. She recorded the location of a thriving stand of red pine and beech that covered the ridge, with trillium and trout lily growing in the shade beneath. Then she scribbled a note in the margin of the drawing, reminding herself to look for the orchids rumored to grow near the lakeshore.

Blue jays chattered, and chipmunks watched with curious interest as she crisscrossed their woodland home, scribbling on the drawings as she walked. She even surprised a big old porcupine as he lumbered through a sunny clearing and, grabbing her camera, managed to capture his escape into the treetops. It would make a great picture, she thought, glad that the prickly fellow had seen her coming before she got too close for comfort.

She walked for miles, back and forth among the trees, meticulously recording every detail. She would have to do the research well if she hoped to make this work. The boys at BFOK, Bristol Foxworth O'Donnell & Kline, were not an easy sell. And twice as stubborn when the pitch came from Rachel. Although they knew full well that her credentials as a landscape architect were impeccable, they persisted in viewing her as the firm's token "tree hugger."

It was so frustrating. She'd made the dean's list in every one of her five years at the university and had interned with one of the best-known firms in the country. They'd have given anything to keep her, but love for Peter had brought her back home again. To Riverdale. And it should have been perfect . . . should have been. She hated to think about how close she'd come to losing everything the two of them had worked for.

Although she'd never admit it to them, BFOK had saved the day. Through sheer determination, Rachel had managed to convince the boys that she'd be more valuable on staff than just on call. "You need a landscape architect," she'd insisted. "It completes the package, everything under one roof." They'd had to agree. The four partners had money, drive, and talent. Engineer, architect, planner, and investment broker, they called themselves development consultants, and specialized in resort planning. They saw Riverdale as the next "boomtown" for the tourist industry, and beyond her expertise, Rachel knew Riverdale. Inside and out, past and present.

The gentle summer breeze suddenly vanished, leaving the air still and heavy with humidity. Puffing slightly from the exertion of the last few hours, Rachel leaned wearily against an old beech tree. It was hard work, trudging through the woods, painstakingly chronicling every interesting little plant, every group of trees, every animal. But she was finally finished, hot and sweaty, and ready for her swim.

"Ladies don't sweat," she remembered her mother telling her. *"Horses sweat. Gentlemen perspire. Ladies get all aglow."* "Huh, I'm certainly glowing today, Mom," she muttered, and imagining she could hear the blue waters of

Quarry Lake calling, Rachel carefully rerolled the drawings and made her way down the hill.

The lake's azure-blue water never failed to surprise her, even though she knew the simple cause. Such a brilliant color, Caribbean swimming pool blue, and all because of the fine limestone dust left behind by the quarrying so long ago. It hung suspended in the water, bending the light, fooling the eye. She felt better already, itchy to take off her shoes, to cool her feet in the refreshingly cold waters. Funny how she could almost hear splashing and childish laughter, an echo of happy times long past.

Turning away from the picture postcard scene, she scanned the little boggy area behind her. "Look for the turtles," Barry Tarr had said, and this, she thought, was where they should be. Piles of sandy rubble, some of them high and dry, made perfect nesting sites for Blandings turtles. Not endangered, but certainly rare, the Blandings had long ago found safe haven in Riverdale Quarry.

Sudden motion and a gentle splash drew her eye, and she followed the line of ripples a little farther along the shore. A big old turtle, his chestnut-brown shell at least ten inches across, stared back at her from the shallows. She'd probably disturbed his siesta, she thought, delighted to discover he'd led her right to the orchids she'd hoped to find.

Dropping to her knees, she touched a fragile bloom with one finger. She'd heard they grew here but had never seen one until today. And Wellman wanted to destroy it all. This was the very spot he'd proposed for the new marina. Hard steel and concrete to obliterate nature's gentle wonders. On the height of land overlooking the quarry, where the osprey now made its home, the lavish main house of Wellman's Riverdale Resort would stand and, ringing the lake, luxury condos, bringing the rich and famous to little Riverdale. But at what cost? So much would be lost, forever. She would have to make them listen. Somehow.

Rachel reached for her camera. Old Man Turtle and the

lady's slippers. It was the perfect shot to finish her roll of film. He seemed indifferent, blinking sleepy eyes in her direction, flashing his bright yellow neck patch just as the shutter snapped. Perfect.

How long had he lived in this peaceful place? she wondered, watching the turtle haul himself onto a sandy hummock. Probably longer than she'd been coming to swim, and that was a very long time. "I won't let you down, old man," she said as he sleepily closed his eyes. "I promise."

Backing slowly away, she left him to finish his afternoon nap. It was her turn for a bit of relaxation now, and she dropped to the ground, eagerly stripping off her shirt with a sigh of relief that the day's chores were done at last. The blue tank top clung to her flesh like a second skin in the heat. She was almost tempted to pull it off as well, but good sense prevailed. Tearing at the stubborn boot laces, she freed her feet, peeled off her sweaty socks *(sorry, Mom, but that's sweat!)*, and plunged her burning feet into the cool comfort of the sparkling blue water.

She stretched, arching her back to release all her pent-up tension, and dreamily closed her eyes. Reaching a lazy hand to adjust the brim of her cap, Rachel let it linger there for a moment, tracing the words RIVERDALE RAIDERS with her finger. Peter's team. Peter's cap, now her trusty companion on every field trip, protected her from sun and rain, and reminded her of him. Not that she needed any reminders.

She smiled to recall the carefree summer days they'd spent here together, and wondered what he'd think of the part she'd been asked to play in its destruction. She wished she could ask his advice, talk it all over with him. If only . . . Sometimes it was so hard to be alone.

Rachel sighed, rolled her head again to loosen the tightness in her neck, and tried to think of nothing but the cool, blue lake. Suddenly something flashed across the water, a burst of light that warned that she was not alone. She grabbed her shirt and shoved her arms into the sleeves. It was inside-out, but she hardly noticed, mesmerized as she was by the flawless physical specimen emerging from the depths.

A man. A man in the water! Almost naked, except for bathing trunks and the watch that blinded her again as the sun reflected off its face. Dripping water, his broad shoulders and back glistening in the sunlight, he stretched and carelessly raked long fingers through his thick, black hair. This was a little closer to nature than she wanted to get.

As he half-turned toward her, she knew with terrible certainty that in another second he would see her, too. Grabbing her camera, boots, and drawings, Rachel scrambled across the narrow beach, her only thought to escape. The stranger might be a maniac, an attacker. And she was the one who'd left the chain down.

She ran, heart pounding against her ribs until she feared it might burst, each breath a ragged gasp. Thank heavens she didn't have to go back through the woods. Her feet were taking enough punishment on the hard gravel.

How could she have been so stupid? She'd let her temper get the best of her, let a stranger onto Wellman's property, let her guard down there by the lake, and had nearly gotten caught. Had the stranger seen her, too? she wondered, shooting a quick glance over her shoulder. No one followed. She slowed her pace a bit.

The trusty old Jeep was in sight but not alone. A very expensive companion was parked alongside, sharing the meager shade. Black, shiny, convertible, and a Porsche to boot. The man might be a maniac, but he was a rich one. She'd never seen a car like that around Riverdale before.

Who cares where he's from? Get in the car and drive! Sprinting the last few yards, she leapt into the Jeep, flinging her armload of drawings and boots onto the seat beside her. One boot, that is. She quickly scanned the path she'd traveled, but could see no sign of the missing footgear.

Go, go, go! But the keys held fast to her belt loop, refusing to obey her trembling fingers. She ripped them free,

8

fumbled with the ignition, winced as the motor chugged and quit. *Temperamental as always, but please, not now. He might be right behind.* Staring back toward the lake, she held her breath and floored the gas pedal, trembling with relief as the engine raced to life.

Leaving the Porsche in a cloud of dust, she sped toward the exit. Who was this almost-naked intruder? she wondered. This blatant trespasser on Wellman land. And it was all her fault! She'd left the chain down to spite Wellman, and wound up spiting herself.

But wait. Maybe there was a way to exact a little revenge on the intruder. Stopping just outside the gate, Rachel pulled the heavy chain across the entrance, smiling with satisfaction as the lock snapped into place. "There," she said, still panting from the exertion of her marathon dash to the car. "Let's see Mr. Hotshot and his fancy Porsche get out of that." It served him right.

Street Wellman smiled. *Hope she enjoyed the show,* he thought, amused but slightly disconcerted. After all, it wasn't every day that he managed to get caught so skimpily dressed, and by a beautiful woman, at that. Grabbing a towel, he briskly rubbed himself dry, taking a long moment to enjoy the sun's warmth on his body.

If Rachel had stayed to watch a little longer, she would have noticed how bronzed, how athletically fit he was. Muscles rippled across his back as he bent to retrieve his jeans and slip them on. No socks. Street Wellman never wore socks—not even in winter.

He eased his feet into a pair of expensive Italian leather sandals but left the shirt off, slinging it over his shoulder in a tangle with the damp towel, carelessly brushing the hair from his eyes to look at his watch. He was running late again.

Life seemed to have slowed its pace in the few days since his arrival in Riverdale. Even so, there was much to be done and he'd indulged himself far too long in the pleasures of this spectacular setting. Taking one last look around, he smiled a satisfied smile. He knew he'd return often, and almost regretted having to share any of it with the rest of the world.

Street let himself enjoy the last few minutes of his visit to the soon-to-be Wellman's Riverdale Resort, strolling leisurely back to his car. He remembered the first time he'd seen the place, under cover of snow. The decision to buy it had been easy once he'd walked the beautiful terrain. It was very different in summer. Even better, if that were possible. He was certain he'd made the right choice.

Something lay on the path just in front of him, something looking suspiciously like a boot. A very tiny boot. He bent to pick it up, smiling again to remember the obvious charms of the young woman who'd made such a hasty retreat from the lake. It had to be hers, he thought, and winced to think of how painful this terrain must have been in bare feet. Still, he'd suffered some surprise and embarrassment himself, only just managing to turn his back before making eye contact. As it was, she'd seen enough. Enough to send her running like a rabbit back to that Jeep of hers. Who'd have ever guessed that such a rusty old relic would belong to a woman? Sandy would find the whole situation quite funny, probably say it served him right.

He dropped the boot unceremoniously into the trunk of his car, tossing the towel in after it and shrugging on the hand-stitched linen shirt over his broad shoulders. He slammed the lid. She'd really made a mess of his freshly polished convertible, and probably on purpose, he thought, surveying its dust-covered interior.

Brushing the dirt from the fine leather of the driver's seat, he slid easily behind the wheel. At least the Ray•Bans were safely stowed in the glove box, away from all this grit. He settled them onto the bridge of his nose, and turned the key in the ignition, giving a satisfied nod as it sprang instantly to life with a low, rumbling growl. Then, spinning the car around, he tore off up Quarry Road, full speed ahead toward the highway.

He saw it just in time, screeching to a halt within inches of the chain, and cursing under his breath. She could have taken his head off with the darned thing! He grinned in spite of himself, imagining her plotting a little revenge for their unexpected and unnerving encounter. Maybe she was the one who'd left the chain down in the first place.

As he stepped from the car, Street made a mental note to have Sandy inquire as to just how many keys were floating around town. Much as he'd like to let the locals continue to enjoy this beautiful place, he knew that Wellman Enterprises would be in deep trouble if anyone was injured on the property. And a lawsuit was *definitely* not part of the plan.

He let the chain fall with a clank into the dust, and hurried to drive through the gate. He'd wasted enough time already, he thought, returning to fasten the barrier, and checking with one last, firm tug to reassure himself that the lock would hold fast.

"Smallville," he thought, ruefully shaking his head as he drove back toward little Riverdale. And they were committed to staying for at least three more years. Had he made the right decision? Sandy would be with him for the duration, no matter what, but Kit? Maybe the place would be just what she needed. Quiet, friendly, and stable. They'd moved around too much in the last ten years, and it had been hard on her. Maybe here she could regain some of that self-confidence that he remembered his little sister having, even at a very young age. Not that she'd ever be the same again, but at least a bit better . . . maybe. He could hope.

Rachel eased her bruised and aching feet into a basin of hot water sprinkled liberally with Epsom salts, and moaned loudly into the darkness of the silent house. Why hadn't she just stayed quiet and put on the boots? Of course, at the time, running had seemed the only possible course of action.

She closed her eyes, willing herself to relax and unwind, but there he was again. The mysterious stranger, bronzed and glistening in the sun like some Roman god. Her eyes flashed open in surprise. What on earth was wrong with her? Was she suddenly some kind of Peeping Tom pervert?

Try as she might, she was unable to wipe the memory of that moment from her mind. He'd been standing there, dripping, as she drove along the highway back to town. He'd been turning toward her, in her mind anyway, as she dropped her film into the night box at the Photomart. And now, in her fevered imagination, he was closer. Much closer. Close enough that she could see the firm muscles of his back and arms, the long legs—like runner's legs, she thought—and the thick mass of black, wavy hair that had fallen across his ruggedly handsome face.

Stop! Handsome? Where the heck had that come from? She'd been too far away to see him clearly. Too far to see all those rippling muscles, too, or anything else of interest. Not that she was interested. Not at all. Really! Realizing, to her chagrin, that she was blushing furiously, Rachel laughed out loud and shook her head, hard, to erase his image. Boy, she'd spent far too long out in the hot sun.

Still chuckling to herself, she turned on the light, wiggled her toes in the hot water, and unrolled the Wellman survey on her lap. It was time to give some thought to tomorrow. This was one meeting she'd better be well prepared for.

Chapter Two

Street Wellman's Porsche was still dusty. For some reason, Sandy had been unwilling to go out at midnight and polish it up for him. Temperamental was the only word to describe his live-in secretary and companion of so many years. Sandy had made one concession, though, getting up a little early to wipe down the interior of Street's prized convertible. The rest would just have to wait.

He saw it even before he'd turned into the driveway off Main Street. In the corner of the parking lot, in the shade of a big maple tree, sat the very same red Jeep that had yesterday been responsible for the mess that now covered his usually immaculate vehicle. Interesting, he thought. Very interesting indeed. He wheeled to a stop beside it, remembering the little lone boot he'd found and that brief glimpse of the lovely woman who'd lost it.

Street grinned to himself as he unlocked the trunk, picking the dusty boot up by the laces and tucking the wool sock back inside. The owner was sure to be very pleased, and grateful, to get it back, he thought with a twinkle in his eye. Especially considering the circumstances under which it was lost. *Yup, bound to be a happy lady.*

He sauntered into the lobby of the old stone building, wondering if perhaps those stones had been quarried from his newly acquired property, back in the early days of Riverdale. It was cool inside, that particular kind of coolness associated with old stone. He liked it. Liked the welcoming yet businesslike flavor of the interior, and he congratulated himself on another choice well made.

The receptionist looked up over half glasses when he entered, a pouf of decidedly artificial platinum blond hair exploding from a purple band tied tight on the top of her head. Her pleasant expression changed to one of puzzlement, though, when she noticed the single boot dangling from his hand.

"Hello there," said Street, perching casually on the edge of her desk.

"Um . . . g-good afternoon, sir. How may I help you?"

"Well," he said, leaning closer, "you can start by telling me who belongs to that little red Jeep out in the far corner of the parking lot."

"Oh, I'm sorry, is it in your way?" She was obviously uncertain of his motives. Street immediately removed himself from her desktop and produced a business card. "No, not in my way. Just wondering. I have an appointment. The partners are expecting me."

The receptionist stared at the card for a moment, then cast a sideways glance in his direction. Not what she'd expected, it seemed. Good. Street liked to catch people off guard. It usually worked in his favor. That was why he'd arrived for this important first meeting wearing faded jeans and sandals instead of a business suit. He adjusted his tie and regarded her, regarding him.

She blushed to the roots of her bleached-blond hair when their eyes met, then seemed to decide that he'd do, after all, and smiled warmly. "Mr. Wellman. Welcome to Bristol

Foxworth O'Donnell & Kline . . . and welcome to River-dale.''

Street laughed, reading her name from the plaque on her desk. "That's quite a mouthful, Dotty. Do they make you answer the phone that way?"

Dotty giggled. "I'm used to it, I guess. Please, come with me. They're waiting in the boardroom. And by the way," she said as he followed her down the hall, "the Jeep belongs to our landscape architect, Rachel Jennings-Porter."

Dotty swung open the double oak doors of the formal meeting room. "Mr. Wellman is here," she announced, with a wave of her hand to show him in. "Will there be anything else, sir? There's fresh coffee on the table, but I'd be happy to make you some tea if you'd prefer."

"Thanks, Dotty, coffee's fine. You've been most help-ful."

Bristol, Foxworth, O'Donnell, and Kline rose in sequence from their chairs around the table, hands outstretched, a gesture of welcome that went temporarily unnoticed as Street locked eyes with Rachel. She'd been gaping at him from the moment the doors swung open, and blushed a deep crimson when she saw what he carried in his hand.

This can't be happening, she thought, toying briefly with the idea of making her escape through the boardroom window. Just yesterday she'd seen the man almost naked, thought he was an attacker or maniac . . . or Roman god.

The partners wore expressions of stunned disbelief as their newest and most valued client crossed the room in three long strides, stopping beside Rachel who sat as though in shock, her face a brilliant red. A single boot dangled loosely from his hand, and once in front of Rachel he raised it high above the tabletop and let go. It struck the polished oak with a resounding thunk, sending a puff of dust into the filtered air of the boardroom and scattering a

15

residue of dried mud and gravel across the table. "Yours, I believe, Ms. Jennings-Porter."

Charmingly straight-faced, he turned to greet the partners. "Good afternoon, gentlemen. Nice to see you all again. Let's get down to business, shall we?"

Without so much as a glance in her direction, Street sat in the closest chair and folded his hands on the table. "What do you have for me so far?"

I know what I'd like to give you, thought Rachel, feeling her blood begin to boil. What gave him the right to embarrass her like that? And then sit there, cool as a glacier, as if nothing had happened. He'd probably blown her credibility with the partners, and what about him? Would he ever take her seriously, given the circumstances of their first "meeting"? Clenching her fists under the table, Rachel willed the red to recede from her cheeks. Her work would be twice as hard now.

". . . slides? Ms. Jennings-Porter? Uh . . . Rachel?" Harry Foxworth's annoying voice cut through the fog, snapping her back to reality.

The slides. "Of course, Harry." She forced a smile. "Pardon me, I was . . . just a little woolgathering, I guess." Rachel allowed herself one quick look in Wellman's direction. His back was turned. Already looking at the screen, waiting to hear what she had to say. And she'd better make it good. This was bigger than her wounded pride. This was for the quarry, for Riverdale.

She took some small pleasure in directing a polite request to Harry Foxworth. "Get the lights, Harry, would you please?" She knew he'd hate that.

Taking her place beside the screen, she cleared her throat and smoothed the front of her dress. Even in the dark, she could feel Wellman's gaze, as real as a touch, and she shifted uneasily, her still slightly swollen feet uncomfortably wedged into a pair of dressy green pumps. Pointedly ignoring the man's persistent stare, she drew a deep breath and began her presentation.

"There's an osprey nest in the top branches of this beautiful old tree," she said, her voice clear and steady, not betraying a hint of the inner turmoil she'd felt since Street Wellman walked into the room. "I only saw the one when I was on-site yesterday, but there's been a nesting pair in the quarry for years. The mate was probably in the nest with their young." She clicked to the next slide, an array of yellow trout lilies.

"Erythronium americanum," she began, and Street let his thoughts wander away from her delicate voice, to the soft curl of reddish blond hair around her face, to her wide eyes, shining in the darkness. It was remarkable how the simple cotton sundress and tailored jacket she wore picked up the dappled greens and yellows of the spectacular slide that flashed onto the screen—as if she herself was part of the forest scene. He found himself wondering if it might be Miss, or Mrs., Jennings-Porter. She certainly made Smallville a lot more interesting, he thought, and then imagined how furious she'd be if she knew what he was thinking. Almost sheepishly, he turned his attention to what she had to say. Impressive. Not only beautiful, but intelligent, too.

She finished her presentation with a slide that brought a quiver of emotion to her clear and gentle voice, a portrait of a rare Blandings turtle, his bright yellow neck patch prominently displayed. With obvious affection she referred to him as "Old Man Turtle," suggesting he might be the quarry's oldest resident. In the background, a cluster of lady's slipper orchids, waxy-white and purple-veined, completed the picture.

Rachel held her breath, and then said it, fully aware of the risk she was taking. "Mr. Wellman, this is the very spot where you propose to build your new marina. If you proceed with the present plans, everything you see here will be lost. *Forever.*" She forced her voice to remain calm. "There *is* a better way."

17

The room fell eerily silent. Rachel bit her lip and waited. Had she gone too far? Had she just lost her job? When Harry hit the lights, every eye in the room was on Street Wellman. Walking slowly back to her seat, Rachel scanned the faces of the partners. Leon was livid. The planner, Stu O'Donnell, looked as if he'd seen a ghost, and Roger Kline had that horrified expression, peculiar to investment broker types, as if he'd just seen several hundred thousand dollars sprout wings and fly out the window. Harry was lounging against the far end of the table, obviously waiting for the other shoe, or in this instance the other boot, to drop. Time seemed to stand still.

"Well," said Street, breaking the silence at last. "We certainly wouldn't want to expropriate Old Man Turtle, or any other of Ms. Jennings-Porter's friends. Perhaps we'll have to rethink the project." He turned to face her. "Did you have something in mind?"

As the partners breathed a collective gasp, Rachel glanced at Leon, who quickly nodded approval. Well, what else could he do at that point? She was on her own. It was time to take a chance.

"A floating marina," she said, mustering all the confidence she possessed. The room stayed silent. "I've looked at the surveys, and I really think it could work. Leon, tell me if I'm wrong, but haven't you engineered a floating marina before?" She knew he had, but waited for him to nod and pick up the ball. The boys took it from there, as she'd hoped they would.

Rachel heaved a sigh of relief as Wellman's steel-gray eyes, and his attention, turned to the four men across the table. She absently brushed a remnant of gravel from the tabletop, and kicked at the prodigal boot beneath her chair. She needed time to think. Wellman had astounded her with his seemingly wholehearted support. She might have to rethink her whole opinion of the man.

* * *

The meeting over at last, Rachel hurried to collect her slides from the projector. Wellman was chatting with the boys at the far end of the room. As their laughter peaked, she wondered self-consciously if he'd told the truth of their meeting the day before. She hated to even imagine the questions the boys would be firing at her, especially the filthy-minded Foxworth. She'd seen the smirk on his face when the boot hit the table, his knowing leer when she blushed in response. Surely Wellman was enough of a gentleman to keep it all to himself. *Oh, no!* The boot slipped out of her hand and hit the floor. She fumbled, nearly dumping the whole tray of slides onto the table. Wellman was looking in her direction, walking slowly toward her. He stooped to pick up the boot.

"I enjoyed the presentation, Ms. Jennings-Porter, and your ideas. You've given us all a lot of food for thought." He paused, a knowing smile playing at the corners of his mouth. "You found some interesting subjects at the quarry yesterday. Did you get any other photos I might be interested in seeing?"

Rachel felt the blush begin somewhere around her waist, spread hotly up past the collar of her jacket, and flash across her face. She saw Foxworth watching with great fascination from across the room, saw the mischievous twinkle lighting up Wellman's cool, gray eyes. "I . . . I . . . that is—" She snatched the boot from his hand and clutched it to her chest like some kind of armor. "I *definitely* didn't see anything else of interest. Nothing worth wasting film on."

Wellman smiled. If only he'd stop smiling, she could stay angry. There was something so charming about him. And he *had* just saved her job. But she knew his reputation as a womanizer, and his ruthless approach to business. She'd have to watch her step with this one. Wellman and Company had a pretty shady past. She would not trust the man, or anything he said, without questioning his motives and intentions.

19

Forcing another smile, she extended her hand, speaking loudly enough to be sure her words would carry across the room. "Thank you, Mr. Wellman. I appreciate your support. We'll do our best to make your resort a success."

Street folded his powerful hand around hers, holding gently but firmly, preventing escape. The heat of his touch flashed up her arm, making the breath catch in her throat. His thumb traced gentle circles on the back of her hand and made her tremble. Did he feel it?

"Excuse me," she said softly, withdrawing her hand, avoiding his eyes, horrified by the sudden fire his casual touch had ignited.

Having no desire to be left standing in the room with the boys after Wellman made his exit, Rachel smiled tentatively and excused herself. He didn't move, giving her no choice but to brush against him in her haste to get away.

She stumbled as the doors swung closed behind her, feeling her heart flutter like a wounded bird in her chest. That second brief touch had been every bit as powerful as the first. She had to get away.

Working up a half-cheerful smile, she forced her feet to carry her down the hall. Dotty stared at the single boot with frank curiosity as she passed, obviously dying to ask what that was all about. Rachel didn't give her the chance. Knowing Dotty, she'd find out anyway, somehow. She always did. "See you tomorrow," she called, and ducked out the door.

Her heart sank when she saw the black Porsche parked beside her little Jeep. No longer the impressively shiny status symbol she'd seen in the quarry, it was now a sorry mess of dust and grime. *Did I do that?* she wondered, wishing for a moment that she could turn back the clock.

Catching sight of Wellman's lean frame advancing on her as she slipped behind the wheel of the Jeep, all regrets vanished. He'd got his revenge with that stunt in the boardroom. "Yes?" she snapped, as it became obvious he intended to start a conversation. "Is there something I can help you with? If not, Mr. Wellman, I'm running a bit late, so . . .''

The man stepped aside without a word, his expression inscrutable, and waved her on her way.

Wrenching open the door of the dusty Porsche, Street threw himself into the front seat, gripping the steering wheel with both hands and gritting his teeth until the muscle in the side of his jaw twitched painfully. He'd come so close to making an apology. He'd even *wanted* to apologize after seeing the panicked expression on her face when that boot hit the table. He hadn't meant to hurt her, but the woman was so exasperatingly stubborn. She'd wait a long time, now, for an apology.

He waited until she'd pulled out of the parking lot, then intentionally turned in the opposite direction, watching in the rearview mirror as she sped along Main Street. He made a quick U-turn as she dropped out of sight, wondering why on earth he'd bothered to go the wrong way in the first place.

Chapter Three

Rachel examined her reflection in the polished glass of the wide front door at Riverdale Place. Clunky white jogging shoes seemed oddly out of place beneath the feminine print dress and tailored jacket, but there was no way she was going to jam her feet back into those green pumps. Absolutely no way.

She sighed, forcing herself to stand up straight and square her shoulders before walking inside, trying her best to ignore the nagging discomfort behind her eyes. Leftover stress, courtesy of Street Wellman? Or was it the wistful pull of the tears she was fighting to hold back? Probably a combination of the two, she decided.

Self-pity, that was all it was. She couldn't let it get the best of her. But so many memories waited beyond the door. Memories that had a way of tugging at her heartstrings, and her tear ducts, usually at the worst possible times. Well, she'd known all along that volunteering here wouldn't be easy. She also knew it was something she had to do, wanted to do. After all, she'd spent so much time here during the last months of Peter's illness that the place felt almost like a second home. And someone new had come to stay, she reminded herself. Reason enough to stop dawdling around on the top step. She pushed open the door and strode briskly inside.

"Well, look who's here!" A high-pitched, cackling laugh made her start and look around. Standing behind her was an elderly lady with a walker and cane. The cane was held high, brandished as if it were a weapon. Either that, or a heck of a good attention-getter, Rachel decided.

"Hi, Mrs. Woolsey. I love your hat."

"This old thing? It's just a little something I picked up in Paris when I was buying for Saks." She frowned. "Well, that must be forty years ago, now. But never mind about me. What about you, dearie? Have you got yourself a nice young man yet?"

Rachel felt one of those annoying blushes beginning to creep up her face. "Now, Mrs. Woolsey, you know I don't have time for dating."

"Oh, pshaw. There's always time for love. You're young and beautiful. There's no reason on this earth for you to be spending all your time alone. Or here with us misfits." She held up a hand to silence Rachel's protests. "No, girl, men and women are meant to be matched up together. It's human nature. Why, I've even got my eye on that new Mr. Parsons." She paused reflectively.

Rachel was well aware that "that new Mr. Parsons" had been a resident for more than two years, and that he found Mrs. Woolsey to be more than a little overbearing, even scary. But she managed to keep a straight face.

Mrs. Woolsey adjusted her hat, setting it even more jauntily askew, as her face assumed a purposeful expression. "Must run, dearie. I just remembered he takes an afternoon stroll right about now. See you later, girl. Oh, Mr. Parsons!"

She scooted toward the door, leaving Rachel feeling more cheerful than she had for days. Coming here was good for her. She could feel the tension dissipating like a fog, banished by Mrs. Woolsey's sunny good humor.

"Rachel, so glad you could make it. We're having one of *those* days today." Head nurse Rina Wickers hurried toward her with short, efficient strides. She held a patient chart in her hand, and was obviously on her way to some person in need of her immediate attention.

"Hi, Rina. Anything you need me to do before I meet our newest girl?"

"No, Rachel, that's fine. You just go on ahead. I told Kit you'd be coming to see her. She's been looking forward to it, I think." Rina hesitated. "Um, Rachel, Kit's in 104. I—I hope that isn't too difficult for you . . ." Her voice trailed off as she bustled away, too busy to consider the situation further.

Room 104. Peter's room. She'd known it would have to happen eventually, but knowing didn't make it any easier.

A raft of feelings flooded through her as she walked toward the familiar doorway, like a sudden downpour on a clear day. Kit, not Peter, was waiting for her at the end of the hall, and that was the way it would be from now on. This wasn't going to be easy. She liked to think that she was starting to heal a little, but sudden reminders let her know that she still had a long way to go before her life would be filled with sunshine again.

Stopping just outside the doorway, she peeked hesitantly around the frame. She could just make out the form, slight and slender, of someone lying on the bed, dangling one leg over the edge and swinging it back and forth in a steady rhythm. So this was Kit. She looked much younger than her twenty-three years, but given the circumstances, that was to be expected.

Lifting her hand to knock gently on the door, Rachel realized that Kit wasn't alone. There was a man with her. A small, meticulously groomed gentleman, formally dressed in a waistcoat and suit pants, with black shoes polished to a gleaming shine. The tiny, perfectly turned-out man was apparently well known to Kit, whose delicate face was upturned, watching with an expression of complete trust and love.

Gently clearing her throat, Rachel took one halting step into the room. The neat little man was in the middle of relating an anecdote.

"And so, my dear, the workmen were so disorganized that Bobby had to ask them all to leave. I, to be perfectly frank, was beside myself with all the mess." He examined his fingernails as if expecting to see a portion of the "mess" somewhere on his manicure, looking up when he noticed Rachel, and darting a protective glance at Kit. "Who might you be?"

"I'm Rachel. I volunteer here, try to help the residents feel at home. I just wanted to introduce myself to Kit." Noting the man's skeptical demeanor, she added, "Really, you can check with the staff."

He smiled, extending his hand. "My dear, I can see that you're perfectly all right, and I am very pleased to meet you, Rachel." He bowed, and firmly clasped her hand in his, giving a brief tug. "Allow me to introduce myself. I'm—"

"Bucky. He's Bucky." A peal of laughter bubbled out of Kit as she bounced happily on the bed. "Tell her you're Bucky, and tell her that Bobby's coming to take me fishing today."

The man smiled gently, even indulgently, at Kit. "That's right, Bobby will be coming to take you fishing. But he said 'soon.' Not today. He'll be in to see you later, but fishing will have to wait a while."

Kit frowned, looking briefly troubled, then almost instantly turned a sunny face to Rachel. "Do *you* like to go fishing?"

"Sure do, Kit. Call me Rachel, okay?" What a sweet child . . . though not a child. She would have to remember that Kit was a young woman. "I have an idea. Why don't we visit the reading room? I'll bet they have some books about fish. Maybe you could show me what you and Bobby like to catch.''

"Now? Can we go now? Is that okay, Bucky?''

"Oh, dear. I've interrupted, haven't I?'' said Rachel. She'd been so charmed by Kit that she'd almost forgotten the little man. "I could come back in a few minutes, if you like.''

"No, no, not at all. I was on my way, and it looks as if the two of you are going to get along like a house afire.''

Rachel watched as the tiny and immaculate man leaned over to give Kit a quick peck on the cheek. As if embarrassed to be caught in a moment of human frailty, he straightened abruptly and adjusted his waistcoat with a firm gesture. "Not to worry, Kit, I'll be back tomorrow with a nice fresh mango for you.'' He rolled his eyes in Rachel's direction. "Not that it seems at all possible to find anything even remotely nice and fresh in the produce stores I've seen since we got here.''

"What about Bobby?'' asked Kit, curling her lower lip into a pout.

"Your big brother said he'd be in to see you later. After dinner. Can you remember that?''

Kit gave a solemn nod.

Ahh, thought Rachel. *Bobby's the older brother. Interesting.* She smiled at Bucky. "Try Martini's, over at Bridge and Pearl. Best fruit and vegetables in town, and their prices aren't too outrageous.''

Bucky studied her closely, as if really seeing her for the first time. "Why, thank you, my dear. How kind. It's difficult to find things when you're in a new place, and I must admit, it drives me to distraction when I can't make a proper meal, or start off the day with a good piece of fruit.''

Such a sweet, funny little man, thought Rachel, biting sharply on her lip to halt the quivering that threatened to erupt into a giggle. No wonder Kit seemed so fond of him. Bucky was quite a character. She blushed to find she was still the object of his studious stare.

26

What an attractive and utterly charming woman, he thought, his matchmaking flair suddenly emerging. *Perfect for Bobby.* Those horrid shoes of hers were a definite fashion faux pas, to be sure, but little eccentricities could easily be overlooked in a person of such obvious substance. And this Rachel was compassionate, too. Very kind. Yes, perfect.

Sighing his approval, he made up his mind, right then and there, to find out everything he possibly could about her. Granted, they'd only just met, but if there was any reason that she was not the perfect match for Bobby, why, he'd eat restaurant cooking for a month. The very thought made him queasy. But Sandy Buchanan never made bets with himself unless he was absolutely certain of the outcome. And this, he felt sure, was in the bag. "Lovely to meet you, Rachel . . . I didn't catch your last name."

"It's Jennings-Porter. And you? Are you a relative of Kit's?"

"No, he's not a relative, he's Bucky," chirped Kit. "He's always Bucky." As if that explained everything. "Can we *please* go to the reading room now? Please, Rachel? I wanna look at the books about fish."

Bucky gave a cheery wave as he clipped smartly down the hall. "Good-bye, Kit, I'll be back tomorrow. And Bobby will be in to see you later."

Kit looked surprised to see him still there at all. " 'Bye, Bucky," she said, holding fast to Rachel's hand and pulling her along the hall in the opposite direction. "Rachel and I have some fun things to do. See ya."

Chapter Four

"I got exactly what I asked for," muttered Street. "Probably not all I deserved, though. What the heck was I thinking?" He kicked at the stones underfoot, replaying the scene in Bristol Foxworth's boardroom as if it were a clip from a bad movie. The horrified expression on Rachel's face when she looked up from her notes and saw him standing in the doorway; the sudden pall that swept away the bloom from her cheeks when she realized exactly what it was that he held in his hand; the crimson blush, the sharp flash of anger in those clear, blue eyes, when he stupidly dropped that darned boot on the table in front of her. A *very* bad movie, indeed.

If only he could turn back the clock. Rachel had probably been a bundle of nerves to begin with, he thought, under the gun to impress with her presentation, and all the while planning to spring that "floating marina" idea of hers. He chuckled. Gutsy lady, that was for sure. It had been obvious that he wasn't the only one taken by surprise by her suggestion. He tried to imagine Leon or one of his partners pulling a stunt like that, and laughed aloud at the notion. Not a chance.

Rachel had chanced it, though. And there was definite merit to her argument. He'd made sure to let Leon know he thought so, too. The man would be hard pressed to find fault with her after that.

But why had she run away? And why had he let her push all his buttons? Nobody got to him like that. Street clenched his teeth at the memory of their confrontation in the parking lot.

Things had certainly not gone according to plan. He'd made some lame excuse to Leon and the boys about being late for another meeting, and rushed out after Rachel, stopping only long enough to extract some vital information from that delightfully odd receptionist.

"Good-bye, Dotty," he'd said, flashing her a charming smile on his way past the front desk. "Thanks for everything, especially that great coffee of yours."

Dotty, obviously underappreciated by her employers, had flushed with pleasure at his compliment, and he'd taken advantage of her momentary confusion. "By the way, is Mrs. Jennings-Porter still in her office? Or . . . is it *Miss* Jennings-Porter?"

Without thinking, Dotty had blurted out the very personal information he sought. "I think Rachel prefers Ms. Her husband passed away, so—" Apparently Dotty's good sense had returned in that instant. She'd eyed him suspiciously.

He'd smiled again, as if he had no interest whatsoever in that bit of local trivia, and then offered an absolutely inspired explanation on his way out the door. "I'm looking for somebody reliable to do a bit of yard work. Thought she might be able to recommend a local landscaper. Would you ask her for me, please?"

He'd intended to offer Rachel a very sincere apology for his boorish behavior, perhaps suggest they have dinner together to make amends. But she'd bristled angrily the moment she saw him in the parking lot, throwing daggers in his direction with those suddenly frosty blue eyes of hers, and letting him know, in no uncertain terms, that she'd rather be anywhere else but there, with anyone else but him.

Street sank woefully onto the rocky beach. Draping his arm across his knees, he stared out across the lake, *his* lake. The surface of the water mirrored the surrounding cliffs and trees, and sparkled with the vibrant colors of sunset. *What a glorious place,* he thought, with a growing understanding of Rachel's passionate defense of it.

He sighed, resting his chin on his hands, and wondered just how much she knew about him and Wellman Enterprises. If he'd been in her shoes, he'd have done his homework. He'd have wanted to find out everything he could about the big, bad stranger who'd just bought a part of Riverdale's history. *Darn.* That probably meant she'd read all the horror stories, knew all about the dastardly deeds of his dear old grandfather Roderick Wellman.

Street knew that his grandfather had never understood the ramifications of his business practices, or the true cost of his own prosperity. He'd run the company for profit, just as all the early millionaires had done, and he'd been very successful. To him, indeed to most people of his era, the earth was a commodity, there to be bought and sold, to be exploited.

Unfortunately, Street's father had grown up believing the same to be true. Things had been done, many things, that a man of good conscience would not have considered. Roderick the Second had, for many years, been obsessed with profit, determined to fill his father's shoes and make his own children multimillionaires. In the seventies and early eighties, he'd begun to see the error of his ways. It was a terrible shame, thought Street, that his dad never had the chance to make things right.

It was all up to him now, and he wondered unexpectedly

if Rachel might be the one who would help him. Lovely Rachel with the icy blue eyes and fiery hair.

Giving a crooked sort of half-smile, Street leaned forward to pick up a flat rock and sent it skipping across the glassy surface of Quarry Lake. Five . . . six . . . seven skips before it sank beneath the water. Kit would never believe he'd done that.

Rachel was totally charmed by Kit Laurence. Her musical chattering about everything and anything that caught her interest was like a babbling brook, soothing Rachel's psyche. How wonderful to spend time with such a gentle, innocent soul, particularly after the day's excitement with the boys at BFOK, and the incredibly arrogant Street Wellman.

Curled comfortably on a couch in the Riverdale Place library, listening to Kit prattle on about her older brother, Bobby, Rachel couldn't help contrasting the two men in her mind. From what she could deduce, Bobby was a considerate, loving, patient, and understanding man. Street Wellman, on the other hand, was cold, calculating, mean-spirited . . . and why did the word "arrogant" keep springing to mind?

Of course, Rachel's conscience niggled her a little when it came to Mr. Wellman. Much as she disliked him, she couldn't deny that he was the most attractive man she'd ever met. Except for Peter, of course. That went without saying. But Peter was gone. It was good that his room now belonged to someone else. Time to put the past to rest, with Kit Laurence's help.

Kit was a bit of a mystery, though. Rachel had checked the patient chart, but it only gave the name and some medical particulars. There was nothing to indicate where she'd lived before coming to Riverdale Place. Odd. There was usually much more personal information available.

All she knew for certain was what Rina had told her. And that wasn't much. Just that Kit had been the victim of a near-drowning accident twelve years ago. And now, at twenty-three, she remained, in her own mind, the same age she'd been at the time of the accident. Eternally childlike.

Kit tugged gently on Rachel's arm. "Can we go for a walk now? I wanna go sit under those big droopy trees near my window."

"The willow trees? Sure, let's go. There's even a swing at the bottom of the garden." A walk in the evening air, wandering around the grounds, would be pleasant, she thought, and she couldn't help smiling as Kit led the way outside. She had designed the landscape of Riverdale Place herself, just a year before Peter had fallen ill. The grounds were special to her in many ways, and she never tired of walking them.

"Rachel, come on!" Kit was tugging eagerly on her arm. "I found the swing. Will you push me? I wanna swing really high." She thrust out her arms, swooping and careening, pretending to be a bird.

The longer Rachel was with Kit, the more she felt that she was in the presence of a lovely, lost angel. Her long, raven hair flew out behind her as she ran, then surrounded her face like a dark cloud when she stopped for breath. Her luminous eyes shone out from behind that cloud like celestial signposts. It was only when trying to make actual contact with the person behind those eyes that one became aware of Kit's confusion.

She was impatient now, running ahead to clamber onto the swing, shouting, "Higher, push me higher. Look, I can fly!"

Caught up in Kit's happy mood, Rachel decided that her day, which had started out and continued to be utterly chaotic, was coming to a most satisfactory close.

"Rachel, I'm tired of swinging. Let's go for a walk, okay?"

"Sounds good, Kit. You can tell me some more about your wonderful brother."

That was all the encouragement Kit needed. She linked her arm through Rachel's as they strolled up the lawn together. "Bobby's the best brother in the whole world," she said, not for the first time. "He always takes care of me—well, Bucky takes care of me, too, but Bobby does fun things. Like fishing. He taught me how to use real bait, just like he does." She looked earnestly up at Rachel. "I even pick up the worms and put them on the hook. By myself. And y'know what? Bobby takes me for drives in his car, too. I already know where the ice cream places in town are." She paused, as if tasting something, then sighed dreamily. "Chocolate ripple . . . mmmm. Do you like ice cream, Rachel?"

"Sure do. Maybe one day, after you're all settled in, we could take a drive together and get some cones."

Kit gave her an enormous hug. "Can we go now? Huh? Can we?"

Oops. She'd have to be more careful what she said. Kit was obviously very literal-minded, likely to take everything she heard right to heart. "Soon, I think, Kit. After you're all settled in here. Y'know, maybe I could help you with that. What kind of things do you have that are still packed away? Any games to play, or pictures we could look at?"

Kit stuck out her lower lip in an instant pout. "My turtles. All my turtles are still in a box somewhere. Bucky promised he'd find it right away." She looked up at Rachel again, her wide-set eyes brimming with tears. "I really want my turtles, Rachel. Can you ask Bucky for me?"

"Well, I'll see what I can do," she said, careful not to promise anything she couldn't deliver. "Let's go see what Rina has to say."

"Oh, Rachel, listen. That's a robin. I *love* robins. Mommy and Daddy loved robins, too. We always used to sit out and have our tea on the balcony and listen to the robins before . . . before . . . oh, I can never remember." Kit rubbed her eyes with both hands, looking for all the world like an exhausted infant.

Before what? Rachel wondered, and resolved to find out. Maybe she would take a trip to see Bucky. She'd taken an

33

immediate liking to the dapper little man, and perhaps she could find out more than just where Kit's missing box of turtles had gone to. "Come on, Kit. Time to go in."

It wasn't hard to convince Kit that a nap before dinner would be a good idea. Rachel helped her get comfortable.

"When Bobby comes," she said with a yawn, "when Bobby comes, you tell him that I . . . I . . ."

Rachel pulled a light blanket up over her shoulders. *Tell Bobby what?* she wondered. *That his little sister fell asleep waiting for him . . . or that I've been waiting a long time to meet someone like him?*

Oh, boy! Where'd that come from? Instant infatuation, and she hadn't even met the man yet.

Tiptoeing out the door, she cast a final glance at Kit, curled up on her bed. There had to be some way to get hold of her belongings and help her arrange Peter's room— no, *her room*—just the way she wanted it. Getting Bucky's address was a likely first step.

The much-pursued Mr. Parsons was sitting in a far corner of the lobby with a hunted expression on his face. He touched Rachel's sleeve as she passed on her way to the nurses station.

"Is she gone?" he asked in a hoarse whisper. "Do you think the coast is clear for me to go to my room?" His eyes darted nervously back and forth, scanning for the enemy.

Rachel patted his arm sympathetically. "I think you're quite safe at the moment, Mr. Parsons. Mrs. Woolsey's probably changing for dinner right now. You have an hour's reprieve, I imagine."

"Oh, thank you. She follows me, you know. She's relentless." He closed his eyes and shook his head. "A man's not safe with that woman around."

"You know, Mr. Parsons, she's really a very sweet lady, once you get to know her. Not all that scary. And she sure likes you."

"Not that scary? Have you looked at her, Rachel? All those wild clothes and crazy hats. Why can't she like someone else? I just want to live a peaceful life."

"Yes, but don't you feel just the tiniest bit flattered that Mrs. Woolsey finds you so irresistible? I mean, there are other eligible men here at Riverdale Place, but *you're* the one she finds so attractive. She may be a little, well, forward, but that doesn't alter the fact that she thinks you're pretty hot stuff."

Rachel sat back, watching Mr. Parsons for a reaction. He was giving what she'd said a lot of thought, she could tell. Finally, he asked, "Is that true? Is that really why she bothers me all the time? I thought she just didn't have anything else to do."

"It's absolutely true. Why don't the two of you take a walk together, or have a game of cards in the social room? I think you might be pleasantly surprised."

"You know, Rachel, you could be right. Maybe I'll just wait here till she comes back from changing. Thank you, my dear."

"You're more than welcome, Mr. Parsons. Let me know how you make out, okay?" She left him pondering his next move.

Rina was making a brief stop at the nurses station, and Rachel hurried to catch her before she took off on her rounds. "Rina, could I have a word with you?"

"Sure. I've got about a minute and a half before I check on the next patient. How'd you make out with our little lost lamb?"

"That's what I wanted to speak to you about. Kit's worried that she doesn't have all of her treasures here with her. Is there any way I can get hold of, uh, Bucky's address or phone number? Maybe I could pick up some of her things. You know, help her unpack them, get her feeling more at home."

"That's a great idea," said Rina, slipping behind the

desk. "Just let me see what I have here for her." She keyed a patient code into the computer and quickly scrolled through Kit's file until she found what she was seeking. "Ah, here it is. It's a Mr. Buchanan you want to talk to. I'll write the number down for you, and you can give him a call. They've just moved to town, so I'd imagine things are pretty chaotic. I bet he'll be glad to have the help." She exited Kit's file and retrieved a chart from the desk, obviously preparing to dash off down the hall.

But what about brother Bobby? Rachel wondered. "Do you know anything about the family, Rina? Anything that might help me make Kit feel more comfortable?" There, she'd covered her tracks quite nicely.

"Sorry, Rachel, all confidential stuff. Gotta dash. Thanks for your help today."

Fine, thought Rachel, pocketing the slip of paper with Bucky's number on it. She would do some sleuthing on her own. And calling Mr. Buchanan was right up there at the top of her To Do list.

Chapter Five

" 'Morning, Rachel."

Glancing up from her computer, Rachel cringed to see Harry Foxworth's familiar, and always unwelcome, smirk advancing through the door. Preceded, as usual, by the overpowering scent of his expensive cologne, Harry sidled into the little office carrying two cups of coffee. *The man doesn't know the meaning of the word subtle,* she thought, wrinkling her nose in distaste as he planted himself in the chair beside her desk.

He was up to something, all right. " 'Morning, Harry," she said with a wary smile. "What's up?"

He slid a steaming cup of coffee across the desk. "Just wanted to see your smiling face, Rach. Double-double, right?"

Rachel turned back to the computer to save the drawing she was updating, then leaned back in her chair, arms crossed, waiting. Harry delivering coffee *and* remembering her preference? A definite first.

"So," he said, trying a little too hard to be pleasant,

"how're the base plans coming along for the quarry? Nearly finished?"

She nodded at the computer screen. "I'll be sending them to plot as soon as this one's done. Leon wants prints to show Mr. Wellman."

"Ah yes, Mr. Wellman. He seemed quite taken with you, Rachel." Harry's lips curled into a suggestive leer. "Seems you two had already met somewhere before the meeting last week, eh? Left some of your clothes at his place?"

Rachel clenched her teeth. If only this once, she intended to avoid blushing over that first encounter with Street Wellman. "He was at the quarry when I did my site inventory, Harry. We saw each other across the lake, that's all. I didn't know it was Wellman until he returned my boot."

"Hmmm." Harry winked. "All right, mum's the word. Still, I think you should try to be nicer to the man. You weren't exactly your warm, caring self, Rach, rushing out the way you did after our first meeting. Anyone would think you were trying to avoid him."

Rachel rose slowly to her feet. It took every ounce of willpower she could muster to keep her voice cool and her temper under control. "Harry, do you actually want something? If not, I'm very busy, so . . ."

"I'll leave you to it then. Although . . ."

"Although *what,* Harry?"

"Well, we were all thinking you might want to ask Mr. Wellman out for drinks, maybe even dinner. A warm welcome to town for the firm's most important client. You know the drill, Rachel."

He laughed at her exasperated sigh. "Now, now, Rachel," he said, his voice taking on a deadly serious tone. "We all do it. Me, Leon, Stu, even Roger from time to time. Good client relations, that's all. Of course," he said as he moved closer to the door, "you have a few talents we don't."

Harry ducked into the hallway just as Rachel's daily journal flew past his head. Picking it up from the floor with an exaggerated "tsk-tsk," he placed it warily on the file cabinet just inside her door, and winked again. "Wear something slinky and short, won't you, Rach? I'd say you're just his type."

Rachel stalked across the office and slammed the door, feeling bested once again by Harry's dirty mind. As if she'd even consider such a thing as outright flirting with a client for business's sake.

In truth, of course, she had considered the flirting part, at least. More than once since meeting the charmingly handsome Mr. Wellman. And now the mere mention of his name gave rise to a vivid memory of that touch in the boardroom, those sparkling gray eyes, that bronzed body rising slowly out of the depths of Quarry Lake.

Okay, Rachel. Deep breath. In . . . and out. In . . . and out. Calm down. She rubbed her eyes, banishing Harry's grating voice and Wellman's memorable face from her thoughts. No matter what, she would be pleasant to the man this afternoon. But there was absolutely no way they'd talk her into inviting him out after work. *No way.* She had a date with the rockery tonight, anyhow. Something had to be done about the weeds in that garden, before it was too late.

Street Wellman stood at the window in what was soon to be his kitchen, drinking a cup of Sandy's English Breakfast tea. It was well past noon, but Sandy hadn't been able to find the Earl Grey. The whole place was in a state of disarray that was slowly driving Sandy to drink, or so he said. And so Street had withdrawn to the peace and quiet of the window. He was trying to imagine how his backyard would look once the work crew had cleared away the construction rubble and that horrible tangle of weeds.

Perhaps, he thought, Ms. Jennings-Porter would agree to design the landscape. It might be very pleasant to get to know Rachel away from the office. Or not. He remembered the angry set of her jaw when last they met, and chuckled at how furious she'd managed to make him. But they'd have a fresh start today, he promised himself, turning to discover the source of the clatter that suddenly filled the room behind him.

"How can I possibly be expected to function in this mess?" Sandy dumped a second box of pots and pans onto the counter, sending half the collection crashing onto the freshly laid tile floor. "If you expect to have a proper dinner tonight, I absolutely *must* have my flan pan!" He stomped angrily out of the room.

Slowly shaking his head, Street began to pick the scattered cookware off the floor, packing it away in the box. No point even trying to put anything into the cupboards. Sandy would say it was all wrong and do it over.

The flan pan had come to rest under the table, beside a tub of tile grout left behind by one of the workmen, and Street placed it wordlessly on the table as Sandy returned to the room.

"Well. You found it. Good." He sank wearily into a chair and allowed Street to bring him a cup of tea. "We should've had all this work done before we arrived, Bobby. People aren't meant to live like this."

Street patted his shoulder. Bobby? The man hadn't called him Bobby for years. He really was upset. "Just a few more days, Bucky. By next week they'll all be finished and out of your way. It's going to be just the way you wanted it, okay?"

Sandy gave a quiet harrumph, and settled into the chair to sip his tea and stare out the window at the river.

"I'd better get moving," said Street, glancing at his watch. "I've got a couple of stops to make before the meeting at Bristol Foxworth. Don't let it get you down, Bucky. It'll all be over soon."

An angry mob closed ranks around Street Wellman's Porsche as he turned into the driveway at Bristol Foxworth O'Donnell & Kline. There were nearly twenty of them, all card-carrying R.A.T.S., waving placards and shouting. Twenty seemed quite a sizable crowd in little Riverdale.

Stu O'Donnell rushed from the building as Street drove up, waving his arms and yelling something unintelligible above the chants of "Save Our Quarry" and "Turtles, Not Tourists."

Street calmly stepped from the car, engaged the alarm, and strode through the front door without a second glance at the crowd. Stu followed, shouting something over his shoulder about private property and calling the police, before nervously slamming the door.

"Mr. Wellman." He gasped, obviously shaken by the unexpected turn of events. "I can't tell you how sorry we are about this. We've no idea how those lunatics knew you'd be coming. But"—and he turned to glare accusingly at poor Dotty—"we *will* find out."

"Don't give it another thought, Stu. I've seen worse." Street smiled reassuringly at Dotty, who was cowering meekly behind her desk, biting her fingernails. "I'm sure no one here is at fault." He slapped Stu soundly on the shoulder. "So, where's your team? Let's get started."

Scarcely twenty minutes later, the crowd surged through the double oak doors of the BFOK boardroom, interrupting Leon's technical explanation of the mechanics of a floating marina. Close on their heels was a weeping Dotty, sobbing her apology for letting them in. "I couldn't help it," she said with a sniffle. "They just pushed right past me."

Barry Tarr stopped at the end of the table, his R.A.T.S. crowding into the room behind him, placards in hand. They stared down the length of the polished oak table at the shocked faces of Bristol, Foxworth, O'Donnell, Rachel Jennings-Porter, and their newest client, Mr. Street Wellman.

Leon's face contorted with rage. "Exactly what do you think you're doing here, Tarr? You can't just barge in uninvited. This is private property. *Get out!*"

Rachel stood. She'd known Barry Tarr all her life.

Maybe he'd listen to reason. She felt her hands tremble and thrust them into her jacket pockets, trusting her attempt at a calm expression would mask the surprise and anger she felt at Barry's reprehensible tactics.

He spoke first, raising his hand to silence the mob. "We want to be heard. Then we'll leave. Not before."

"Call the police, Dotty, *now!*" ordered Leon.

"Wait." Street Wellman's steady voice stopped Dotty in her tracks. "Let's hear what they have to say, Leon. We can spare them a few minutes, I think."

Rachel sank back into her chair, gazing across the table at the man who seemed so endlessly full of surprises. When he caught her eye and winked, she was completely taken aback. Was he trying to make her blush again?

"Right. You've got ten minutes, Tarr. Make it good." Dropping heavily into his chair, Leon picked up a pen and began to doodle on the page in front of him, a clear message that nothing they might have to say could possibly be worth hearing.

Barry cleared his throat. "The quarry is a way of life in Riverdale. More than that, it's a unique habitat that isn't found anywhere else in this region. Your development will destroy all that, wipe out an amazing variety of species. Blandings turtles, for example. They're quite rare."

Mutters of agreement rumbled through the R.A.T.S. as Barry took a deep breath and continued. "This is *our* town, Mr. Wellman, not yours. You think you can make a lot of money here. Well, maybe so. But then you'll run, leave us with a bunch of noisy tourists, and none of the things we all hold dear. We're ready to fight. Whatever it takes. And we figure you've got a right to know that, from the start."

Stu O'Donnell was on his feet before the words were out of Barry's mouth. Watching him lurch across the room, Rachel feared he'd had one too many over his lunch at the Dog & Biscuit, and wished that for once Harry would do the right thing and stop his partner before he made a fool of himself. No such luck.

"You can't tell somebody what to do on his own land, Tarr. Mr. Wellman's invested a lot of money in this town. Use your heads! Think of the jobs and benefits to Riverdale. All your property values will rise. Considerably. Do you R.A.T.S. want to jeopardize that for a couple of frogs?"

Rachel cringed. Stu had really blown it this time, she thought, watching the faces of the crowd grow angrier. And Wellman just sat there. Was he spineless, or what? Somebody had to do something.

"Please, listen to me," she began, not at all sure what she'd say next. "You all know me. Barry, you know what I stand for, what I believe in. We don't have all the answers yet, because we're still studying the options, but I can promise you this. As long as I'm involved in this project, the protection of the turtles and the habitat that supports them is every bit as important as the marina, the condos, and the developer's bottom line."

Someone behind Barry grumbled, "We'll believe that when we see it."

"I'm working very hard to show you," she answered quietly. "And so far, Mr. Wellman has been very supportive." She gave him a sideways glance, hoping he'd stand up for himself, say something on his own behalf, but no. He sat quietly, acknowledging her with a barely perceptible nod.

"Rachel?"

She turned to face Barry again.

"It's true. We've all known you for a long time. And you've never lied to us before. But don't think you can pull a fast one. We'll be watching."

"No fast ones, Barry. As a matter of fact, we were just discussing dates for a town meeting. Mr. Wellman wants everyone to have a chance to comment on the proposal. And we'll be listening. It's a promise."

Dotty pushed open the doors and stood aside as the R.A.T.S. filed out of the boardroom and down the hall. No

43

one spoke until they heard the lock click shut on the lobby door.

"Well done, Rach!"

That was probably the first kind thing Harry Foxworth had ever said to her, and Rachel had no idea of how to respond.

"*Very* well done, Ms. Jennings-Porter." Street Wellman's deep voice sent a chill up her spine. She turned slowly to face him before he spoke again. "I'm certainly glad we've got you on our side."

The partners laughed, leaving Rachel to wonder just how she should interpret that remark. Did Wellman intend to follow through on his promise to protect the quarry habitat, or was it all just smoke and mirrors?

He leaned over the base plans, pointed an elegantly long finger at an area close to the lake, and laughed heartily at some witty, probably lewd, comment by Harry.

Rachel felt utterly abandoned. She'd done their dirty work again, got them out of a really sticky situation with Barry and his gang, but she still wasn't certain of Wellman's motives. She felt incredibly relieved when he glanced briefly in her direction and suggested they adjourn for the day.

"We're all a little rattled. Enough's enough. Let's go home."

Chapter Six

It seemed there were more weeds than flowers in the gar den this year, a lot more. Rachel rested on her heels amo the struggling clusters of perennials in the rockery. Sh been at it for nearly two hours, and had barely made a d in the bumper crop of thistles, purslane, and burdock threatened to obliterate the carefully planted hillside.

"Oh, Peter," she whispered, "how could I have get this bad?" She sighed, fighting back tears at the th of him. It seemed like only yesterday that they'd pl this hillside, scoured the property for rocks and bou wrestled each one into place, nestled tiny sprouts and between the stones. A labor of love.

By their third summer at The Willows they'd h reward. The garden had burst into bloom with c yellow, white, and purple—even before the last s melted, and carried on with an endless succession and fragrance until first frost. That had been Pe summer.

Rachel sniffed, swiping tears off her face wi glove. She missed him so much. It was all so u

Bracing her foot against a boulder, she began a fierce tug-of-war with an enormous burdock. It wouldn't budge. *"Let . . . go . . . you . . . ohhhh, no!"* The weed gave way, tumbling her backward down the slope. She came to a painful halt with her back wedged against a sharp rock, bare arms buried in a mass of thistles. For one split second, her world faded to black.

Rachel hadn't heard him run across the yard, the sound of his footsteps drowned out by her own shout. And so the strong arms that suddenly embraced her, sweeping her out of the dirt to hold her tenderly close, came as quite a shock. Such a shock that, for a moment, she imagined Peter had somehow come back to rescue her. Or maybe that bump on the head had been harder than she thought. *Could this be heaven?* she wondered, as he rose to his feet, cradling her safe in his arms. *No.* The warmth of his breath in her hair, and the pounding rhythm of his heart, told her this was all too real.

She moaned as he turned toward the house, sending blue sky, clouds, and trees spinning wildly, a dizzying kaleidoscope of color. Rachel wrapped her arms around him and squeezed her eyes shut, trying hard not to faint. Dropping her face into the hollow of his neck, she breathed deeply. He smelled of sandalwood and leather and, when he spoke, his voice rumbled through her body.

"Rachel? Are you okay? That was a bad fall!"

Her eyes flew open as Street Wellman deposited her gently on the porch swing, and dropped to his knees in front of her.

"You!"

"Me?"

"What are you doing here?" she demanded, wincing as he dabbed at her bleeding elbow with an expensive, monogrammed handkerchief.

"I wanted to thank you for handling that situation with the R.A.T.S." He cupped his hand firmly around her arm,

46

applying steady pressure on the now-ruined handkerchief to stanch the bleeding. "You see, Riverdale only knows me by reputation. Not necessarily all true, I might add. And since we're all going to be neighbors . . . well, I didn't feel I should be confrontational." He grinned. "Ms. Jennings-Porter to the rescue. I couldn't have done better myself. Thanks."

A worried expression took shape on his face before she could reply. "Rachel, we should clean this up. It's a nasty scrape, and you're breaking out in welts from the thistles."

He laughed then, pulling a burr from her hair and brushing the tangled mess of curls away from her face. "I'm sorry," he said, his face frozen in a grin that suggested he wasn't really sorry at all. "For laughing, I mean. But you should look in a mirror."

Brusquely pushing his hand away, Rachel struggled to her feet and tottered toward the door. Wellman's tautly muscled arm materialized around her waist again, uninvited and unwanted, but she let him support her for fear of falling. She was feeling dizzy, and not at all sure she could make it to the kitchen on her own.

"Witch hazel," he said firmly as he eased her onto a chair at the kitchen table. "That's what we need to soothe those welts. Where would I find it?"

Rachel stared up at him blankly, feeling bruised and battered, and wishing he'd just go away and leave her to die. Of embarrassment, if nothing else. She'd caught a glimpse of herself in the mirror as they crossed the hallway. Street Wellman certainly had a knack for catching her at her absolute worst.

Her face was slightly sunburned beneath the tear-streaked layer of garden dirt, giving her a permanent and, she thought, most annoying blush. Bits of twigs and leaves clung fast to the ratty tangle of hair that hung limply around her shoulders. Her arms were scraped and bleeding, covered top to bottom with burning, itchy welts that grew larger, redder, and hotter by the second, begging to be scratched. And Street Wellman wanted witch hazel?

"I don't think . . . I haven't got any witch hazel," she said, wondering how on earth the man would know about such an old wives' remedy. He looked at her as if no home could be complete without it.

"Well, we'll just have to make do then. Baking soda?"

Rachel pointed to the cupboard above the sink, and watched as he filled a basin with cool water, sprinkled in a handful of soda, and placed it carefully in her lap. She found herself studying him, admiring his broad shoulders and the wave of dark hair that fell over one eye as he leaned toward her. Even the way he moved was impressive, so confident and graceful. A surprising contrast to his height and powerful build.

He turned, crossing the room again to pull a clean towel from the drawer, as if he'd visited many times before and knew exactly where such things were kept. Then, Street Wellman, the great and powerful man of quarry-wrecking and turtle-slaughtering fame, knelt before her on the kitchen floor and, ever so gently, began to bathe her arm.

Rachel shivered as the cool water splashed onto her T-shirt. Too much sun again, she thought, as Wellman turned his attention to her other arm. He seemed intently focused on what he was doing, and she sensed he'd had some experience in this kind of "taking care." His movements were naturally gentle, and she couldn't help but enjoy how it felt to be touched by those hands.

She shivered again when he looked up at her and smiled. A rush of feelings, long forgotten, stirred deep within her as he ran those long fingers through her hair, brushing it away from her face before carefully wiping the grime from her cheeks with the cool cloth. A steady dribble of water fell onto her shirt, trickling down her front. Rachel felt herself responding to his touch against her better judgment.

"I'll do that," she said, snatching the towel from his

48

hand. "I—I'm feeling much better now, and . . . and I can't thank you enough for being so kind, Mr. Wellman."

"Rachel, please, call me Street. We're neighbors now, after all, and friends, I hope." He lifted the basin from her lap and took the towel from her hands before she could stop him, turning quickly away to set them in the sink.

"Where's your first-aid kit? We should cover that scrape." He bent to examine her elbow again. "It's still bleeding."

"Please, don't bother." Her throat tightened. "I . . . I'll have a bath first and then . . ." For Pete's sake. What was wrong with her? Why couldn't she think straight?

Street smiled as if he knew exactly what she was thinking. "You feel very warm, Rachel. Too much sun, maybe? We'd better get you something to drink. Tea?"

At least the man knew when to change the subject. "Something cool, I think. There's fresh lemonade in the fridge. Would you like some?" Rachel tried to stand, but found she couldn't. She sank back onto the chair with a groan.

Street knelt swiftly by her side. "What's wrong? Where does it hurt, Rachel?"

"It's nothing," she lied. "Just a bruise. I think I remember landing on a sharp stone."

His gentle hands had lifted the tail of her T-shirt before she could object. "Your back has a nasty bruise, Rachel."

She leapt to her feet, ignoring the pain, spinning away before Street could stop her. As she stared at him, mortified, he strode purposefully out of the room.

I've offended him now, and he's leaving, she thought, shocked to find herself wishing he'd stay. She leaned weakly against the table, preparing herself to follow, to say good-bye and offer a proper thank-you for his kindness. He was back at her side before she could set her feet in motion, draping an afghan around her shoulders and guiding her backward onto the chair.

His arm lingered around her for a moment and she had

to fight the impulse to lean against him, to breathe that wonderful musky scent again, to experience those strong arms around her in a passionate embrace. Then he was gone, rummaging through the refrigerator, pouring lemonade into two glasses, returning to sit across the table looking terribly concerned, and incredibly handsome.

"I think you should see a doctor, Rachel. I don't like the look of that bruise."

Rachel sipped her lemonade. "I'm sure it's nothing. I'm just a little stiff, that's all. Some aspirin and a good night's sleep is all I need, Street."

She smiled as she spoke his name. Street. It suited him, but she couldn't help wondering what kind of parents would name their child after a roadway. Perhaps it was a family name, a fashion of the rich and famous.

Street was studying her seriously from the other side of the table. He didn't seem convinced that she was really all right. Well, she wasn't entirely convinced herself, but she appreciated the fact that he didn't argue with her. Surprisingly enough, she was beginning to respect Mr. Street Wellman. Respect, with the added bonus of physical attraction. She wondered if he felt the same longing when they touched.

"I have to ask, Rachel. What on earth were you doing up in that weed patch? You were yelling at the top of your lungs when I drove in. I thought you had some wild animal cornered, or something."

She hung her head, feeling another rush of guilt over the dreadful condition of Peter's beloved rockery. "It's not supposed to be a weed patch. It's our rock garden. My husband and I planted it together, babied it along for two years while it got established. It was beautiful last year, Street."

She blinked and swallowed hard, determined not to cry. "After Peter died, it—" She caught herself, and just in time. No need to confess the dire financial straits, how there'd been no time to worry about weeds, how, for a while, every minute of every day had been a battle to keep from losing the land they grew on. "It's just so much to take care of. The house, all the gardens. I didn't realize how bad the weeds were until— It would break his heart to see it like this." She sighed. "I'll keep at it, a little at a time. Maybe one of the kids from the high school will help out. There's always somebody looking for part-time work."

Street nodded. "Good idea. It's too much for one person, Rachel. You really could have been badly hurt, you know."

"I guess I'm lucky you arrived when you did, Street." It was amazing how easy it now seemed to call him by his first name. She resisted the urge to reach across the table and touch his hand. "If not for you, I might still be lying out there."

He nodded, glancing quickly at his watch. Was she keeping him from something important? Perhaps a business meeting, or dinner? It had to be nearly eight.

"I'll be fine now, Street." She tried to sound strong and cheerful. "You don't have to stay and baby-sit me. Really."

"Well," he said, looking down at his watch again, "I really should call home. Sandy's probably waiting dinner."

Sandy? The man was married! Or living with someone. She felt as if she'd been kicked in the stomach. How stupid she'd been. Alone for so long, thinking she was just fine, making it on her own. But the first man to come along and touch her managed to fill her mind with all sorts of wild imaginings. *Grow up, Rachel!*

She drew a deep breath. "There's a phone in the hallway, Street. Please, go ahead and call home. I feel just awful to think your wife might be worrying about you."

"My wife?" Street laughed, a big, booming guffaw that bounced around the room making her smile in spite of herself. "Oh, my. That's a good one, Rachel. Be right back."

He left her feeling incredibly foolish, wondering what

51

was so terribly funny about the thought of being married to Sandy. Didn't the man believe in marriage?

"Rachel," he said, rushing back into the kitchen a few seconds later, "if you're absolutely certain you'll be all right, I should go. Seems those R.A.T.S. were at the house this afternoon, marching up and down out front, making a scene. Sandy's pretty shaken up."

"Oh, Street, what an awful welcome to town. I'll be fine, really. You should be at home now, not here."

She walked to the door beside him, careful to keep her distance. No point in any more dreaming about Street Wellman. He was obviously spoken for.

Street stopped in the doorway, turning to take her hand in his. "My card's on the kitchen table, Rachel. If you need anything tonight, anything at all, just call."

Withdrawing her hand, Rachel did her best to smile, telling herself that his interest was just neighborly concern, nothing more. Still, she couldn't help wondering if Sandy knew the powerful effect her man could have on other women. "I'm sure I'll be fine. But thank you for everything, Street. And please, tell Sandy that not everyone in Riverdale is a R.A.T."

She looked so small and alone. Street waved as he turned down the driveway and imagined he could feel Rachel's twinge of pain as she gingerly raised her arm to wave back. She was very lucky she hadn't been seriously injured tumbling down that steep slope. It could have been worse. Much worse.

He paused at the end of the lane to read the hand-painted wooden sign that swung lazily in the evening breeze. *The Willows,* it said. *Rachel and Peter Porter.* "The competition is a ghost," he said with a groan, gripping the steering wheel a little too tightly, remembering how it had felt to hold Rachel safe in his arms. Her tiny hands and delicate features had captivated him. And her trembling response to his touch had fired his own excitement, making it nearly impossible, but absolutely necessary, to leave her.

Gunning the engine, Street wheeled the Porsche out onto the highway. He smiled to imagine Sandy's reaction to the news that he'd finally found someone who really interested him. Not just another golddigger, or social climber. Sandy would like Rachel Jennings-Porter. Street was certain of it.

Sandy grinned at him across the dinner table. "It's about bloody time, my boy." He chuckled. "I was beginning to think I was going to have to devise some devious, yet brilliant, scheme to get the two of you together."

"You've met Rachel?" Street knew he shouldn't be surprised. Within days of their arrival in Riverdale, Sandy Buchanan had visited every interesting shop, introduced himself to the top ten on the Who's Who list, and made the acquaintance of every gossip in town. He had a real knack for listening, without ever giving anything away. A valuable talent, and one that he kept in top form through constant practice.

"Kit introduced us." Sandy let that statement stand on its own, watching the quick succession of surprise, concern, and confusion flicker across Street's face.

"Kit?"

"Your lovely Rachel is a volunteer at Riverdale Place. Kit thinks she's wonderful, and"—Sandy nonchalantly polished his fingernails with his napkin, watching Street's reactions over the rim of his glasses—"I'm tempted to agree with her." He smiled. "Your sister just blossoms when Rachel's around. They get their heads together and chat like old friends. You wouldn't believe it."

"But Rachel never mentioned anything . . ."

"Of course not. She's got no idea that Kit Laurence is your sister. Kit talks about her brother Bobby, and how he's coming soon to take her fishing. You'd better do something about that, I might add. And she introduced me as Bucky. I doubt Rachel would make the connection between

53

Bucky Buchanan and your 'wife,' Sandy.'' He laughed. ''So now I'm the 'little woman,' am I? Hmmm. How quaint. Perhaps I'll try my hand at a little nagging.''

''Oh, please. You don't need any practice in that department.'' Street stood, pacing away from the table to stare out at the big willow in the backyard, and the pair of mallards with their brood drifting down the Mawr River. It was beginning to rain, a gentle, steady shower that would probably last through the night. Rachel was likely standing at her window, watching the weeds grow.

''Are the gardeners coming tomorrow, Sandy?''

''I suppose. If the rain stops. Although how you expect me to get anything done with them here, I don't know. Always traipsing through the kitchen for drinks of water, or to use the phone, or the loo. Dirty, sweaty lot.''

Street laughed. ''Don't bother trying to fool me, old man. There's nothing you like better than a chance to lord it over the workmen. Tote that barge, lift that bale. I can hear it all now.'' He crossed the room to sit at the table again, accepting another cup of coffee. ''Send the workers over to Rachel's place tomorrow. Tell them there'll be a bonus for them if they can get the gardens in shape before she gets home from work. Especially the rockery. And tell them to be careful. I want it perfect for her, Sandy. Picture perfect.''

Chapter Seven

"'Morning, Dots. How's everything today?"

"So far, so good, Rachel." Dotty glanced furtively down the hall and whispered, "Mr. Wellman's here. What a hunk! Just the sort of man I'd pick to take me away from all this."

Me, too. Rachel made a little inward groan. She'd nearly said that out loud. What the heck was she doing? Street Wellman was not available. Not married, true, but there was obviously a serious involvement with this Sandy person. *Get a grip,* she told herself firmly. He was a client first, a neighbor second, and *nothing* more than that. There. That sounded good. Of course, making herself believe it was something else again.

Dotty sighed loudly. What on earth had she just said? Something about Street being the world's most eligible bachelor? *Oh, boy.*

"I wouldn't be too sure about the 'eligible' part, Dotty. He mentioned someone named Sandy. I think they're living together, but you didn't hear it from me." Sandy! Of course. That's what she'd do. Find a way to meet her, maybe become a friend. That ought to put things in perspective.

Dotty frowned. "Sandy? Well, I took a message for him from someone named Sandy, but . . ."

"But what?"

"Oh, nothing. She just sounded very . . . well, husky. Maybe she's got a cold or something." Dotty's face fell into a pout. "Gee whiz! The great ones are always taken."

Rachel mustered all the enthusiasm she could. "Never mind, Dotty. Your Mr. Right is out there somewhere. He just hasn't found you yet."

Feeling suddenly foolish, thanks to her own schoolgirl reactions to Street Wellman, Rachel hurried down the hall to her office and shut the door firmly behind her.

Keeping her mind on work seemed impossible. She fidgeted in her chair, still stiff and aching from her tumble down the hill, and craving, even more than usual, that first cup of coffee. But coffee required a trip down the hall, past the partners' offices and the meeting room. Past Street. Coffee would have to wait, she decided. *Concentrate.*

Wellman's town meeting was set for Monday night and there was much to be done. Her first assignment was to design an eye-catching handout that would, in Leon's words, "Win them all over to our side." In one page, no less! She grabbed two handfuls of hair and tugged sharply. "Aarrghhh!"

It was painfully obvious. No coffee, no work. Time to stop hiding. Taking a deep breath, she walked purposefully across the little office and out into the hallway. No sign of Street. Rachel pushed away the momentary twinge of regret that she'd missed seeing him.

In the kitchen, she stared pensively out the window, stirring cream and sugar into her coffee, and wishing the day was over. Leon and the boys were hassling over something across the hall, their voices raised as if in anger. She tried her best not to listen. It was none of her business, after all.

But the next words out of Roger Kline's mouth shot down every good intention.

"I don't like the sound of this, Leon," he said grimly. "A man like Wellman doesn't need investors. Have you looked at his financial statements? No? Well, I'm telling you, he's got the capital to pull off a project three times this size without new investors. He's stalling—sandbagging."

Rachel slipped into the hallway, hoping against hope that she wouldn't be caught eavesdropping. She recognized Leon's voice next, and held her breath, straining to catch every word.

"What do you suggest I do, Roger? It's Wellman's project. If the man wants to change his mind . . ."

"It makes no sense." Harry paced the room as he spoke. Rachel could hear the heels of his expensive boots tapping an anxious rhythm on the hardwood floor. "Why bother to go through with the town meeting at all?"

"Like I said, Harry, the quarry project is Wellman's baby. He's keeping his options open, I guess." Leon's conciliatory tone of voice was totally out of character. "Don't worry. Whatever he decides, we'll be in on it. He dropped some hints about another big project in the works, too, and he seems convinced that the vote in the town council will go our way. Just keep the man happy. Whatever it takes. And nothing he said leaves this room. Agreed?"

Too strange, thought Rachel, hurrying back to her office. What on earth was Street up to now? Suddenly she felt cold. And angry. The more she thought about what she'd overheard, the more convinced she became that it could only mean one thing. Wellman was going to flimflam the town. He'd be at the meeting on Monday with guarantees of jobs and prosperity, sweetened with promises of saving the turtle habitat. Then he'd just go ahead and build the resort his way. Riverdale would join the long list of towns that had been abused by Wellman Enterprises.

Her hands trembled as she sat at the computer. This was

going to be one spectacular handout. She'd make Street Wellman look like the savior of Riverdale Quarry, friend to the people and protector of the environment. Let him try to wiggle out of that. Barry Tarr and his R.A.T.S. would have it all in writing. And she'd be there, in the thick of it, to back them up.

Chapter Eight

"Hello there, dearie. Come to watch the fun?" Mrs. Woolsey bore down on Rachel at a frightening clip, brandishing her cane in greeting. "We're about to have our first-ever ballroom dancing class. I decided to dress for the occasion. How do you like the outfit?" She turned the walker around slowly, so that Rachel could drink in the sight. Her "outfit" consisted of a strapless, deep purple evening gown, with a maroon bolero jacket and matching pillbox hat. Her shoes spoiled the effect a little, as she was wearing slip-on brown moccasins, for comfort as well as for safety's sake.

"You look fabulous as always, Mrs. Woolsey. Where's Mr. Parsons today?"

Mrs. Woolsey made a disgusted face. "Men! No taste for anything new or different, most of them. Not that we should hold that against them. We ladies will have a fine time on our own. Ahh, but, speaking of men, I've got my eye on a real prime specimen for you, girl. A real hunk of a man. The kind of man I'd like to sink my teeth into . . . if I still had any." She winked wickedly. "You just missed

59

seeing him, too. He left with that nice Mr. Buchanan, not five minutes ago. Don't you worry, though, I checked him out for you. And I *definitely* wouldn't kick him out of the house . . . if you know what I mean.''

"Honestly, Mrs. Woolsey—"

"You're blushing, dearie!" She cackled with obvious delight. "Oh, I do so enjoy seeing that color rush to your face. Only thing is, it should be a man bringing that flush to your cheeks, not an old retired fashion maven like me." She cackled again. "Still, someone has to do it, so I guess it's my job until we get you hitched up with Mr. Hunk. Your little friend, Kit, can introduce you . . . did I mention he's her brother? Looks to me like he's single. And so kind. The way he watches out for his little sister—why, you couldn't ask for a better, more compassionate soul. He's all you deserve, my dear. And more.''

"Well . . . uh, thanks, anyway, Mrs. Woolsey, but . . . I'm doing just fine the way I am."

"Pshaw! Don't you worry, dearie, I'll fix things up for you yet. I've caught a man or two in my day. Why, I could tell you stories— Hey, don't start without me!" With a roar, she scooted across the hallway and into the social room, just in time to find a partner for the first dance.

Rachel waved at the woman's retreating back and breathed a sigh of relief. Thank goodness *that* conversation had been cut short. Not that she minded the vivid firsthand description of Bobby, but a pleasant fantasy about the man was one thing; getting "hitched up" was entirely another. She really wasn't ready to get involved. Not yet. Men were just too confusing. Strong arms and gentle gray eyes could make you feel things you weren't supposed to feel. Want things you had no business—

Him again! For heaven's sake, was it not possible to have a five-minute stretch without thinking of that thorn-in-the-side Street Wellman?

Rachel poked her head around the doorframe of room

104. Hopefully Kit would be awake and feeling like company. "Kit? It's Rachel. Kit? Are you hiding?"

A lump of panic formed in the pit of her stomach and leaped upward into her throat. *Calm down,* she told herself. There was no reason to panic. Not yet. Kit was probably off with one of the other residents, having a wonderful time, not even thinking that anyone might be looking for her. And she couldn't have gone far. Bucky had just left, not five minutes ago, according to Mrs. Woolsey.

A nagging doubt stuck in her mind, just the same. Looking quickly around the room, she noticed how neatly Kit's bed was made, how her books lay perfectly square on the night table. It didn't feel as if she'd been there for some time. Rachel felt increasingly uneasy.

Only one thing to do, she thought, and that was to find Rina as quickly as possible. The whole thing was likely a figment of her overactive imagination. At least, that was what she kept telling herself as she ran down the hallway to the nurses station.

"Where's Rina?" she said with a gasp, startling the petite brunette woman behind the desk. "I need to speak to her."

"She's in 112, giving a patient some physio. I thought you were visiting Kit today, Rachel. What's wrong?"

Forcing herself to remain calm, she said, "Yes, Jan, I *was* supposed to be visiting Kit. The only problem is, Kit is not in her room. And I know she's not at the dance, because I would have seen her on my way in. Has she gone outside with someone, do you know?" Rachel struggled to keep her voice from rising to a shout. Something was not right, she just knew it.

"Are you sure?" asked Jan, obviously concerned. "She was there, waiting for you. I saw her right after her visitors left. She was really excited—something about some turtles she wanted to show you. Oh, never mind that, we have to find her."

"I'll check the grounds," said Rachel, calmer now that

she was taking action. "You check inside. Surely she can't be very far away."

The look of panic on the young nurse's face did nothing to reassure Rachel, but she headed for the door regardless, past the din of big band music and whirling dancers, and down the front steps, scrutinizing every face and every piece of furniture. Every pillar. Maybe Kit was playing some kind of a game. The only problem was, she hadn't bothered to tell anybody the rules.

Out on the lawn, Rachel took a very deep breath. What was the first thing to do when you lost something? Remember where it was the last time you saw it. In this case, the lost item was a human being, but the logistics were the same. Feeling that she was on the right track, she picked up her pace and headed for the willow grove.

At first she thought that maybe her logical thinking had been way off base. There was no sign of Kit near the willows, or on the swing that hung from the old maple tree. Shifting her glance to the top of the ravine behind Riverdale Place, she saw a fluttering movement. Was something lying on the ground? Someone? Rachel ran. *Please let her be all right. Oh, please,* she prayed. The words pounded in her brain with every step. She was almost afraid to look at the frighteningly lifeless form that lay at the top of the hill.

"Kit!" Was she breathing? Blue shirtsleeves, carelessly unbuttoned, flapped gently in the breeze. Drawing closer, she heaved a sigh of relief. Just asleep. She looked so totally angelic lying there on the grass that Rachel just stood for a moment, catching her breath and waiting for her heart to stop pounding. Looking up, she uttered a small prayer. "Thank you. If ever someone deserved a chance, it's this dark-haired angel of yours."

Dropping to her knees, Rachel rested her hand on Kit's arm and called again. "Kit? Wake up, honey, it's Rachel."

Kit's eyes opened slowly, taking a few seconds to focus on Rachel's face. Her expression was one of puzzled surprise. "Rachel? How'd you get here?" She sat up suddenly. "How'd I get here? Where am I?" She looked around in sudden fear, a deer caught off guard in a clearing.

"It's okay, honey. You must have gone for a walk while you were waiting for me to get here, and then you must have fallen asleep. Gosh, Kit, your shirt and pants are all wet from the damp ground. But you're okay. Come on, let's get you back to the house. Everyone's looking for you." She helped the still-confused Kit to her feet and began leading her back to the main door.

"But, Rachel, I was having such a good time with Bobby and Bucky. Then I thought I'd walk to the fishing hole and I was all by myself. I don't know what happened." She turned troubled eyes on Rachel and shivered.

"Come on, Kit, let's go and find Rina. We'd better tell her about your little adventure. You know, honey, it's not a good idea to go for walks all by yourself. I mean, what if somebody wanted to come and visit you, like I did today? Then they wouldn't know where to find you and you might miss out on some fun stuff. You wouldn't want that to happen, would you?"

Kit thought about that as they made their way to the door. "No," she said finally, "I guess I wouldn't. I never thought—" She stopped in her tracks. "Do you think Rina's gonna be mad at me, Rachel?"

"No, of course not. She'll probably just ask you to always tell one of the nurses if you have something you want to do by yourself." Rachel knew there would be far more concern than that over Kit's little expedition. It was sheer luck that she'd fallen asleep while still on the grounds. She could have wandered for a very long way before anyone had spotted her. *If* anyone had spotted her. Rachel slipped her arm around Kit's shoulders. "Look," she said as she led her up the front steps, "there's Rina now."

"I'm sorry, Rina." Kit clung to Rachel's side, her bottom lip beginning to quiver. "Please don't be mad at me . . . okay?"

63

"I'm not mad, Kit. But I'm very glad that Rachel was here to find you. We've been terribly worried, you know."

"I—I know. Rachel told me. I didn't mean to fall asleep, honest, I didn't. I'm *really* sorry." She looked earnestly into Rina's face. "Please don't tell Bobby. He gets so worried about me . . ."

Rina patted Kit gently on the shoulder, winking at Rachel as she took over the responsibility of getting the lost lamb back into the fold. "Don't you worry about Bobby now. Everything's fine. You just have to make sure you always tell somebody if you decide you want to go somewhere. Can you remember that, do you think?"

"I know I can remember, Rina, I really can." Pulling away, she skipped down the hallway that led to her room. "Yucky . . . I'm all wet. I'm gonna change my clothes and then I'll find my box of turtles so Rachel and I can put them away. Okay?"

The two women regarded each other in silence. There was no need to say what both were thinking. Kit was a menace to herself. The young woman floated through her days, totally oblivious to time restraints and the practical considerations of life . . . well, the lives of regular people. She would have to be watched with extra-special care. Losing Kit forever was suddenly a very real possibility.

Rachel was the first to speak. "Look, Rina, I think I can take on some of the burden of keeping an eye on Kit. She and I have a kind of bond that . . . I can't explain. We just . . . connect. Maybe I could give her my home phone number. That way, she can always call me or have someone here call me, if she decides she really wants to do something or go somewhere."

Rina frowned. "Oh, Rachel, we can't possibly ask you to do that. It's a huge responsibility. As if you don't have enough to do already."

"Nothing more important than Kit. She's very special, Rina. Please, let me help."

Rina laughed wearily. "Okay, Rachel, you win. Go ahead and give her your number. You have my blessing."

"Thanks." Rachel hugged the woman impulsively, then headed down the hall toward Kit's room.

"Oh, and Rachel—I know Kit's family will be very grateful," called Rina. "I plan on telling them what you did today, you know."

"Whatever, Rina. The important thing is that she's back and she's okay. I'd better hurry or I'm going to get heck for taking so long."

"Hi, there," said Rachel, peeking through the doorway. "What're you doing?"

Kit was sitting in the middle of her bed, warm and dry in a cozy pink sweat suit, surrounded by mounds of tissue paper. She looked up, smiling radiantly. "Look, Rachel, Bucky brought my turtles. I've got them all unpacked and I put the box under my bed. Wanna help me put them in the case?"

Did she want to help? No question whatsoever. "I sure do, honey. Let's get started."

Chapter Nine

" 'Help Wanted—Long Hours, Backbreaking Work, Low Pay.' That should have them pounding down my door.'' Rachel's chuckle had a melancholy ring to it, and she sighed wearily, trying to coax a bit more speed out of the old Jeep. Just a few more minutes and she'd be home.

If only she'd made the time to write something up and post it at Whitman High. Surely someone was looking for an after-school job.

" 'Lonely widow-woman needs youthful muscle for endless toil in her garden.' '' She chuckled again. At this point, she knew it was either laugh, or break down and cry. She feared she wouldn't be able to stop if she gave in to the lure of tears.

Snap out of it! Turning off the highway at The Willows, she yawned widely, then scolded herself. Tired or not, there'd never be a better time to tackle that rockery. The soil would be nice and soft after the rain last night.

As the shady lane gave way to open lawn and a side view of the house and gardens, Rachel's foot hit the brake pedal, hard. No longer an overgrown tangle of grass and dandelions, the lawns were neatly manicured and edged. The flower beds surrounding her white frame house, only hours ago a sorry mess of weeds, had been transformed. Lupines and columbine, in glorious bloom, stood tall against the porch, with a border of violets nodding happily at their feet.

She strolled toward the garden shed, a rustic affair of barnboard and glass, her eyes wide in amazement at the glory of the poppy garden nestled at its side. She had tried not to look at it for the last few weeks, all those lovely blooms hidden by long grass and burdock leaves. Rachel touched the delicate, papery petals and shook her head in wonderment. "How . . . ? Who could have done this?" She half expected the old shed to answer. After all, the place was obviously under some sort of magic spell. A talking garden shed wouldn't seem too out of place.

Eager to see the rockery, she rounded the corner of the house at full speed, and tripped over a squatting intruder. "Yikes!"

"Whoa! Hey! It's just me, Rachel. It's okay!"

"Danny? Oh, Danny. I . . . I'm so sorry. I didn't know you were here. Are you all right?"

"Never better. Although my ears are still ringing from that whoop you let out." He finished bundling a mass of branches and tossed them into the back of his truck. "The rest of the crew left a few minutes ago. Quite a job, but it turned out pretty nice, if I do say so myself." Danny grinned at her. "Of course, your designs are always beautiful, Rachel. Just like you."

She blushed. Danny Minelli had never tried to hide his infatuation, even back in the days when she and Peter were first married. "Forget the flattery, Danny. There was nothing beautiful about this place when I left it this morning."

Rachel gazed for one brief, joyful moment at her carefully weeded rock garden, before turning to stare at Danny, the "magician" responsible for the remarkable metamorphosis. "What the heck are you doing here?" she demanded.

He shrugged. "Just being neighborly?"

Oh, no, you don't, thought Rachel, picking up on the inflection that turned his statement into a question. This went way beyond neighborly. Either Danny was up to something, or . . . the Wellman job!

"Look, Danny, I recommended you to Mr. Wellman because he asked about a local firm who'd work hard and do a good job at his new house. But this"—she waved her hand at the now-perfect gardens and lawns—"this smacks of a kickback, Danny, and we've had that discussion before. You know how I feel. It's unethical. If I recommend you for a job, Danny Minelli, it's because I respect the work you do."

"It's not like that!" The pained expression on Danny's face confirmed he was telling the truth.

"Well?"

He grinned. "Believe me, Rachel, I'd love to take all the credit, maybe let you wine and dine me in gratitude, but it wasn't my idea. I think you've got an admirer."

"Who . . . ?" *Oh, no!* Rachel tried to close her mind to the possibility that Street was behind all this. Talk about unethical. It put her in an impossible position. What could she do? Insist that Danny put all the weeds back? "Who told you to do this, Danny?"

Shaking his head, Danny backed away, edging toward his truck. "I'm not supposed to say."

"Don't you dare get in that truck!" Rachel caught his sleeve. "You're not going anywhere, mister. Not until you tell me who's behind this."

"Hmmm, held prisoner by the very lovely Rachel Jennings. I can think of a lot worse fates." He shook his head. "You *are* beautiful."

"Danny. Please. We've been friends too long . . ."

"And friendship can lead to love," Danny whispered, lightly brushing a curl of reddish hair from her face.

Rachel pushed his hand aside, stepping quickly beyond his reach. "Who hired you to do this, Danny?"

"Aw, gee. I just blew it, didn't I?" Shoving his hands deep into the pockets of his dusty overalls, Danny grinned sheepishly. "Does this mean you won't have dinner with me?"

Rachel stared at him, her blue eyes flashing a hint of the frustration she felt. The man was exasperatingly stubborn. All things considered, though, dinner with Danny was not an entirely unappealing prospect.

Lounging against his shiny green pickup, he absently brushed a streak of grime from the logo emblazoned on the door. MINELLI LANDSCAPING, it said in white script that encircled a graceful elm tree. He hung his head and scuffed at the ground with the toe of his boot, looking up at Rachel with an endearingly bashful grin as he twisted his ponytail. He had worn his long brown hair that way ever since high school. *You grew up on me, Danny Minelli,* she thought, imagining those broad shoulders of his, shirtless and sweaty.

"You're blushing, Rachel." He laughed. "There must be hope for me yet."

"Not a chance, mister, unless I get the truth. *Now.*"

"Well . . . you didn't hear it from me, okay?"

She nodded.

"It was him—Wellman. We were supposed to start work at his place today, but when we got there he said there'd be a big bonus if we cleared out before you got home. Guess I blew that, too, eh?"

Speechless, Rachel turned her back on Danny and wandered across the lawn, stopping beside the lush border of daylilies, abloom with russet-orange flowers. The delicate scents of lavender and thyme wafted down the hillside on the afternoon breeze. Mounds of yellow alyssum spilled over rock ledges, a brilliant contrast to the ruby-red dragon's blood that nestled in the crevices. Not a single weed remained.

Street. She nudged at a rock with her toe. Just yesterday he'd come to her rescue, sweeping her away off this very spot. She could almost feel his strong arms around her again . . . his gentle hands comforting . . . arousing dangerous, forbidden longings. She shivered uncontrollably.

"You okay, Rachel?" Danny touched her hand, then slipped an arm around her shoulders.

"I . . . I can't believe he did this."

"Well, strictly speaking, he didn't do this. I did."

Rachel smiled up at him. "You did a wonderful job, Danny. Absolutely perfect."

"Thanks. So . . . what about dinner?"

What about dinner? She looked away and sighed.

"It's been a long time," said Danny tenderly. "Too long. Pete wanted you to live life. He told me that, Rachel. Don't hide yourself away. It's—"

"Don't," she whispered. If he said another word, she'd end up crying, and then . . .

"Dinner would be lovely, but not tonight. Call me, okay?"

Slipping her arm through his, Rachel led him across the lawn to his truck. It felt right, she thought. Comfortable. They had a history together. Yes, dinner with Danny might be just the thing to put an end to the disturbing visions of Street that had begun to haunt her dreams. Perhaps Danny Minelli would prove to be the generous dose of reality she so desperately needed.

R.A.T.S. Well, who else would be pounding so angrily on the front door? Street left his coffee on the kitchen step and loped through the side yard, halting at the corner of the house to catch a glimpse of the intruders. That old rattletrap Jeep of Rachel's sat catty-corner across his driveway, as if to block any attempt at escape on his part. *Uh-oh. Now what?* he wondered, as she hammered on the door again.

Rachel nearly jumped out of her skin when he appeared

70

at her side. "I was just thinking about you," he said. "Is something the matter?"

"I . . ." She felt her eyes grow wide. The man was wearing nothing but his blue jeans and watch. "You . . ." She couldn't seem to look away from the narrow vee of hair that graced his broad chest.

"Oh, gee." She closed her eyes. Did he really expect rational conversation while he stood there half naked?

"You're upset about something," he said, stating the obvious. "Please, come sit. I was just having some coffee."

Red-faced, Rachel followed him around the corner, wading through the tangle of long grass and weeds that encroached on the flagstone path. *Nice body.* The thought sprang to mind unbidden. *Oh, yikes!* Was she turning into Harry Foxworth? Why not just whistle and give him a pinch?

"Sit," he said, indicating the back step as he disappeared into the house. Rachel sat.

"Cream in your coffee?" asked his disembodied head, thrust suddenly out the window.

"Yes, please. Sugar, too."

He vanished again, only to reappear a moment later with two steaming mugs of coffee. He'd found a shirt, and shrugged it on as Rachel watched, buttoning it slowly and shoving the tail into his jeans before he sat beside her.

"Sorry," he said, "I wasn't expecting company."

Rachel sipped her coffee in silence, avoiding the gray eyes that now watched her so intently.

"Are you going to tell me what's wrong?" he asked, reaching a hand toward her.

Rachel jumped when his gentle fingers touched her arm, sending a splash of hot coffee onto Street's bare toes. Springing instantly to her feet, she spun to face him, ignoring the wince of pain that flickered across his face.

"It was totally inappropriate of you," she announced, feeling the color rise in her cheeks. "Much too generous.

71

Accepting gifts from clients is not something I'm comfortable with, Mr. Wellman. But this is hardly something I can give back, is it? You've put me in an impossible position, I'm afraid, and I don't know what to do about it."

"Rachel," he said, sighing deeply, as if her anger caused him greater pain than mere scalding coffee, "you needed some help. We're neighbors. Friends, I hope. I helped. That's all."

"That's not what people will think."

"And we're worried about what people will think, are we?"

"It's a small town. People talk. But it's not just that. It's . . . it's not ethical for me to take gifts from a client. The firm has rules about . . ."

Watching him woefully shaking his head, Rachel felt a twinge of regret at her ungrateful behavior. "I . . . it was very thoughtful of you, Street," she said, sitting beside him on the step once again. "I thought I'd died and gone to heaven when I saw the place. It's perfect. But . . ."

"But we need to make it respectable, is that it?"

She nodded.

"All right. Here's the deal. Sandy and I are at odds over this backyard, over the whole property, for that matter. We need some help."

"It'd be my pleasure to help you and Sandy with a master plan, Street." She smiled agreeably. "It's a wonderful property, real potential."

"It's a deal then? We trade your gardens for mine?"

"Deal," she said firmly, taking his hand to shake on it. "I should go—no, please don't get up. I'll find my own way out. And thank you, Street. Thank you *very* much."

"So? What's wrong?" Sandy pushed up his sleeves and snapped on a pair of latex gloves, extracted from a generous supply kept under the kitchen sink. "Don't shake your head at me, young man. You haven't said two words since I got home. Why, you sat right there listening, without a single complaint, through my glorious rendition of 'Des Colores.' And I must warn you, I feel 'Guantanamera' coming on. Can't make a proper paella without the mood music, you know. Oooh! 'La Bamba'!'' Sandy danced across the room, hips jerking in rhythm with his best Richie Valens imitation. *"Arrrribaa!!!"*

"Enough, already." Street grimaced. Unfortunately, music to Sandy Buchanan's ears was not necessarily music to the rest of the world. "Can't hear myself think."

"Too much thinking going on, if you ask me. Which, of course, you didn't," muttered Sandy, dropping a package of fresh shrimp into the sink.

"What's that supposed to mean?"

"Oh, nothing. Nothing at all," the little man replied, wrinkling his nose in distaste as he peeled and deveined the shrimp. "Only that, maybe, a little less thinking and a little more action on your part . . ."

"Would do what, exactly?"

"Would have the lovely Rachel in your arms, instead of running as fast as she possibly can in the opposite direction. Still letting her believe you've already got a woman in your life? The very lovely 'Sandy'?"

"Rachel jumped to that conclusion all by herself. I have no idea what she believes, to tell you the truth. She came storming over here this afternoon, ranting and raving . . . how dare I be nice to her! Seems to think people will get the wrong idea, and that I've somehow put her in a difficult position at work." Street shook his head forlornly.

Sandy was much more interested in the heart of the matter. "But how did she like her gardens?"

"Said she thought she'd died and gone to heaven. But she had me wondering how to put it all back the way it was, for a while. We finally came to an agreement." Street chuckled. "You're going to *love* this!"

"Do tell, dear boy," urged Sandy, vigorously washing the shrimp under running water. "What wonderful idea am I about to fall in love with?"

"Ms. Jennings-Porter has agreed to design the gardens for us."

"Splendid! Oh, I *am* pleased, dear boy. When do we start? Why not invite her over for dinner this weekend?"

"No. Leon's got the whole team scheduled to work, Rachel included. It'll have to wait until after the town meeting, I'm afraid."

Sandy feigned a pout as he stirred a pinch more saffron into the rice, then let a mischievous smile play at the corners of his mouth. "I overheard a very interesting conversation today, about our Rachel."

"Really? And I suppose you're going to repeat it, word for word."

Sandy shrugged. "Well, if you're not interested . . ." He pulled a round, freshly baked loaf of bread from the oven, snapped off one of his gloves, and rapped sharply on the loaf with his knuckles, smiling at the hollow sound it made. Done to perfection.

Street folded his arms. "All right. What is it?"

"This was my manicure day, dear boy." Sandy yanked off the other glove to properly admire his nails. "Marge's Cut 'n Curl isn't exactly the sort of facility I'm accustomed to, but she does do nice work. And you wouldn't believe the things those old biddies talk about under the dryer." He chuckled. "Of course, I just sit quietly by, minding my own business."

"Of course."

"I swear, they're like hungry sharks circling. One of them drops a name, and everybody better watch out. It's an absolute feeding frenzy."

"And just who 'dropped' Rachel's name, I wonder? As if I don't already know."

Sandy tried his best to look aghast. "Well, I might have said something about the lovely young woman I met out at Riverdale Place . . . anyway, the point is, everybody loves her. Not a mean word from any of them. Such a tragic figure, they all say, such a sad romance. I swear there wasn't a dry eye in the place.''

Street shifted uneasily, watching as Sandy added shrimp and vegetables to the simmering rice. ''You're going to make me beg you to tell me, aren't you, you old—''

''An old-fashioned love story, my boy. The real thing. Rachel was the girl next door, and her Peter was everyone's favorite. To hear Marge's ladies tell it, he was the best teacher the world ever knew. They had a fairy-tale wedding on the riverbank out at The Willows. Everybody thought there'd be babies right away, but it never happened. Then Peter fell sick. I don't think anyone really knows what the matter was. Someone said cancer, another leukemia; somebody else insisted there'd been a terrible accident. Anyway, they all disagreed. It's been nearly two years now, and they say Rachel still seems so terribly sad. There was some talk about fixing her up with an eligible young man, and it seems there are quite a few of those in Riverdale. The old girls couldn't agree on who'd make the best match.'' He chuckled. ''You weren't in the running, by the way.''

Street stared moodily at the bottom of his empty coffee mug. ''Huh. Guess not. I'm the evil stranger, right?''

Briefly studying Street's dejected expression, Sandy took pity and kept his considerable collection of Wellman gossip to himself. ''Haven't heard a word about you, my boy. *Nada.*''

''Right.'' Street stood, rolling his shoulders to relieve the tension left over from Rachel's visit. ''I'm going for a walk,'' he said flatly.

''Well, don't go far. Your dinner's nearly ready.'' Sandy shook his head and sighed as the door fell shut behind Street. ''Don't think too much, my boy,'' he whispered. ''You'll think, and think, and think, while the really important things in life pass you by.'' He let himself smile. ''Guess I'll just have to make certain that at lest one really important thing comes looking for you. Ah, Rachel. What to do? What to do?''

Strange day, thought Rachel, climbing wearily into bed. She'd walked every inch of the property, twice, and hadn't found a single weed. Not a stone out of place in the rockery. Not a plant in need of attention. Peter would have approved, she thought, suddenly feeling as if the weight of the world had been lifted from her shoulders. And all thanks to Street Wellman.

Strange man. Her feelings for Street had run the gamut from desire, through distrust, anger, and warm gratitude, coming to rest in a sort of gray area of indecision. After Monday's town meeting, she hoped the truth of his intentions toward Riverdale and the quarry would be known. Then maybe she'd be able to make up her mind about him, once and for all.

A spontaneous image invaded her thoughts. Street, bare-chested and shoeless. She blinked him away, thinking instead about her promise to have dinner with Danny Minelli. Groaning, she pulled the pillow over her head. Was she ready to try dating again? Even with safe, comfortable, familiar Danny? She tried to picture his face and couldn't. But Street was there again, smiling warmly, his gray eyes sparkling with a come-hither shine. ''Go away!'' she commanded. The phantom Street just laughed.

Chapter Ten

Rachel's hands seemed determined to tremble, keeping time with the hummingbird pace of her heart, and she gripped her clipboard a little tighter. Stage fright. But that was the least of her worries. Nearly three hundred people had crammed themselves into the church hall, all looking for answers from Street Wellman. And where was he?

Hovering nervously in the wings, she scanned the familiar faces in the crowd. Neighbors. Friends. People she'd known all her life. That's what it was all about. Community. Her stomach twisted. Was she being used? Just a pawn in Wellman's game? She'd be walking a fine line for the next few hours.

"This handout is great stuff, Rach. Ever thought of getting into politics?" As usual, Harry Foxworth's hand lingered too long on her shoulder.

Don't let him get to you, she told herself, forcing a smile. "Glad you approve, Harry. Mr. Wellman wanted to make a good impression. Hope I did him justice."

"Well, from what I understand, Wellman loves it. But

then''—Harry's upper lip curled—''I doubt you could do any wrong as far as he's concerned.''

''He's seen it?'' she asked, ignoring Harry's distasteful suggestion.

''Huh! You don't honestly think anything made it this far without his approval, do you?'' He gestured grandly toward the stage, pointing to his personal contribution, a beautifully rendered three-dimensional drawing of Wellman's Great Lodge. Nice work. Too bad the man himself was so obnoxious.

''Where is Mr. Wellman, Harry?''

''Talking to the mayor, I think. I'll be sure to let him know you want him, Rach.''

''Don't bother.'' She turned her back, hoping Harry would take the hint and get lost. For once, he did just that.

''All right, people, let's do it!'' Leon's voice boomed confidently as he strode past her onto the brightly lit stage, followed closely by Harry, Stu O'Donnell, and Roger Kline.

''Rachel?'' Street squeezed her elbow. He was so close she could feel his breath on her neck. The touch made her knees weak. *Why now?*

''You'll be fine,'' he whispered. ''You know what they say about stage fright . . . keeps you on your toes.''

Stage fright? She'd forgotten all about that. At least he didn't suspect the truth. She hurried to her seat, brushing still-trembling fingers down her arm to end the lingering awareness of his touch, barely aware that Mayor Carver was at the podium, calling the meeting to order.

Across the stage, Street seemed cool and unflappable in his tailored linen shirt and chambray pants. Smart man. ''Dress to impress'' wouldn't work in Riverdale. He'd dressed to fit in. She saw him nod a greeting to the crowd, then take his seat without a word. Only then did she begin to hear the mayor's gravel-voiced greeting.

''. . . join me in welcoming you to Riverdale. This resort of yours is going to breathe life into our little town and for that, I thank you. I know we're all impatient to hear what your team has to say. They've certainly given us some wonderful images of things to come." A smattering of unenthusiastic applause followed his acknowledgement of the plans and drawings that ringed the stage.

Mayor Carver directed his next comments to Barry Tarr and the R.A.T.S., easy to spot in their green "Save Our Quarry" T-shirts. "I hope we'll all have the good sense to keep this meeting civil. Everyone will have a chance to speak their mind."

Barry nodded as a flurry of signs took to the air. "Turtles, Not Tourists," someone yelled.

The mayor sighed audibly. "Without further ado, I'll hand the meeting over to Leon Bristol, President of Riverdale's own Bristol Foxworth O'Donnell & Kline. He'll give us a bit of background. Leon?"

A buzz of conversation coursed through the room as Leon took his place at the podium. *He's looking quite dapper,* thought Rachel, remembering Dotty's whispered confidence that he'd gotten himself a brand-new suit for the occasion. New shoes, too. They squeaked as he stepped up to the microphone.

"Thank you all for coming. Mr. Wellman's Riverdale Resort is an important new beginning for our community, and we're certainly pleased to see such an outstanding turnout tonight."

Rachel listened thoughtfully to his well-rehearsed speech. He outlined the proposals, neatly avoiding sore points and contentious issues. Very slick, she thought. He wasn't giving them anything they didn't already know. Let the drawings sell themselves. How many times had she heard that advice from him?

"Of course," he said in closing, "the environment is important to all of us, and we're prepared to do whatever's necessary to protect it." Smiling, as if he honestly believed he'd managed to put their fears to rest, he asked, "Any questions?"

79

Barry Tarr was first on his feet. "I have a few." The questions followed, rapid-fire. He asked about the town's water supply, about sewage treatment, traffic, pollution, even the effect of motorboats on Quarry Lake. Turtles wouldn't have a chance against propellers, he claimed.

Rachel heard her own words coming out of Leon's mouth. "We're still studying that. We don't have all the answers. We're working on it."

"Yeah, sure!" someone shouted from the back of the hall. "Y'all know exactly what the darned building's gonna look like, but you don't have a clue what you're doin' to this town. We have to live here, Wellman!"

Suddenly people were on their feet in every corner of the room, demanding to be heard. Leon pointed to an elderly gentleman dressed in overalls and a plaid shirt. "Mr. Butler? You had a question?"

"Not a question, young man, but I do want to say my piece." Len Butler cleared his throat. "There's a lot of us here who've lived in Riverdale all our lives. We love this town the way it is, and we don't want to see it change." The crowd applauded. "I say 'no' to Wellman Enterprises. Take your resort somewhere else!" Len took his seat to another round of applause and cheers.

The next speaker took the floor almost immediately. Rachel cringed. It was worse than she'd thought. She was beginning to suspect there was no one with anything even remotely positive to say about the project, when Dub Taylor leaped to his feet, demanding attention with a wave of his hat.

"Good day. Dub Taylor, Taylor Renovations. Most of you know I've been outta work for the last six months. Riverdale's my home, but I'm gonna have to pack up and move if things don't turn around. I've gotta support my family. This resort could keep me and a lot of other folks busy for the next three years."

Shouts of "Yeah, Dub" and "You tell 'em" peppered the air.

"It's all well and good for you R.A.T.S. to worry about a few turtles," Dub continued, "but I worry about my kids. I don't want them to see their dad taking handouts."

Barry stood. "You'd rather give them pollution, crime, and drugs?"

Oh my gosh, thought Rachel. *Crime and drugs? Where'd that come from?*

"You're the undesirables here, Tarr," yelled an anonymous voice. "You and your R.A.T.S."

Leon hammered on the podium, anxious to regain control. "This isn't getting us anywhere, people. Does anyone have something constructive to say?"

The room fell silent as Dr. Hughson made his way to the front. There was scarcely a person in Riverdale who didn't know and respect the kindly, gray-haired doctor. Many, including Rachel, had been brought into the world by his hands.

"I've watched this town grow for the last sixty-three years," he said, "and I know the problems facing people like Dub, but the quarry means so much to this town. It's a part of us." The crowd waited.

"I'm not against growth. I want new jobs. But if we don't have clean air and water, then what have we got? Just more people? How do we make sure we're doing the right thing?

"This town has always grown slowly. If we made mistakes, we made little ones, and learned from them. Barry? Your own father filled in a wetland to build the house you grew up in. I wonder how many turtles were lost because of that?"

Dr. Hughson didn't wait for a response from the red-faced Barry Tarr. "What I'm saying, Barry, is that we learn from past mistakes." He looked directly at Street. "Well, nothing this big has ever happened in Riverdale before. How can you be sure you're doing it right?"

To Rachel's amazement, Street got up and strode calmly to the podium. Leon made way for his client.

"Like most of you, I really don't understand as much as I'd like to about how we humans affect our environment. That's why I've got professionals working for me—for *you*—to make sure we do the best we can." He glanced quickly at Rachel, as if to warn her of what was to come.

Don't do it, Street. He wouldn't put her on the spot, would he? Beads of perspiration prickled across her upper lip and she was suddenly aware of how warm the auditorium had become. To her dismay, most of her painstakingly crafted handouts had been folded into paper fans that fluttered restlessly in sweaty hands. Even worse was the uncomfortable result of all that random motion. The crowd became a sea of paper waves that rolled toward the stage in endless swells, until the floorboards seemed to pitch beneath her feet. Fighting nausea, she closed her eyes for a second, but only for a second, before Street spoke her name.

"Many of you know Rachel Jennings-Porter. For those of you who don't, I can tell you that she's the landscape architect who's been looking into the environmental issues at the quarry. Perhaps she can offer a bit more information. Rachel?" He beckoned her to the podium.

The stage seemed suddenly very wide, and Rachel wondered if she'd ever reach the center. Street waited, patiently smiling encouragement, making room for her to stand at his side. As the warmth of his body and the compelling scent of his sandalwood musk enveloped her, Rachel grabbed the corner of the podium and held tight. "I see you've all put my handout to good use."

Friendly laughter rippled across the room.

"Hopefully you had a chance to read it first. If not, I hope you'll take it home and give it some thought. As Leon said, we're studying the options for the quarry. But none of us are biologists or ecologists. We'll be bringing in specialists to help us figure out the best possible scenario." Rachel's voice rang clear and true across the now-silent hall. "Mr. Wellman has assured me that he intends to take whatever measures are necessary to protect the unique habitats found in Riverdale Quarry.''

She glanced up to find him nodding agreement. ''Perhaps he'd agree to a second town meeting, once we have more answers.''

Street nodded again. ''Good idea, Rachel.''

''Sounds like a good plan to me,'' growled Mayor Carver, who'd joined them center stage. ''Let's adjourn for tonight. I think we could all use some fresh air.''

''Well done,'' said Street quietly, and turned quickly away to pump the mayor's hand. Rachel wished she could disappear. The look on Leon's face proclaimed his opinion of her little speech, and it wasn't good. Hurrying offstage, she passed close enough to overhear some of his angry diatribe to Harry Foxworth. ''. . . complete waste of time and money. We had the council vote locked up, according to Wellman, and that man knows the ropes. We're going to have to put a leash on our Rachel, I think.''

Greeting her neighbors as they left the hall restored Rachel's belief that she'd done the right thing. Many of them thanked her. Even Barry stopped to shake her hand and say he was glad to know she was on the job. She tried not to dwell on Leon's vitriol. After all, Street had agreed with her, and he was the client. Of course, she'd pretty much put him on the spot. But if he was trying to put one over on the people of Riverdale . . .

Rachel pasted the smile on her face and continued to shake hands until the hall and the parking lot were nearly empty. The cool evening breeze felt so good, but it was time to face the music, she thought, and trudged back down the aisle.

''Good job, Rachel.'' Leon's terse delivery suggested he'd rather be saying something quite different, but his client sat nearby, watching. Rachel wondered what had transpired while she'd been at the door.

''Thanks, Leon. I hope I didn't speak out of turn. It just seemed the right thing to do.''

"Well, I hope it was, Rachel." Leon seemed to shake off his bad humor. "It's been a long haul, people. Thank you all for giving up your weekend to put this together. I'd say we all deserve to sleep in tomorrow morning. See you at noon." He strode offstage and into the growing darkness.

"What's gotten into him?" Harry laughed. "A half day off? Will wonders never cease."

"Sounds like a good reason to lift a pint," said Stu as the group strolled toward the door. "Who's coming to the Dog & Biscuit? Rachel? Mr. Wellman? Will you join us?"

"Thanks, Stu," said Rachel, "but I'm exhausted. Maybe another time. I'll see you all tomorrow."

"I'm expected at home, gentlemen," said Street. "But thanks, and enjoy your morning off. You all deserve it."

They parted company at the front door, with Harry, Stu, and Roger Kline taking off toward downtown at a brisk pace, as if their thirst was growing by the minute. Rachel was left with no choice but to walk through the parking lot with Street.

"Lovely night," she said quietly. "It's a shame we didn't have the meeting out-of-doors. It was so hot in there."

"Maybe we should plan on it next time. Although it would probably guarantee a rainstorm."

"Here's my car," said Rachel, hesitating. "Street, I . . . I'm sorry if I put you in a difficult position tonight. I shouldn't have suggested another meeting without asking you first."

"Don't give it another thought. These meetings are the best public relations tool we have, and I for one am very pleased with the way it turned out." Street reached to open the Jeep door. "Good night, Rachel."

He jogged off across the parking lot, leaving her to ponder the many faces of Street Wellman. Who was he, really? Ruthless developer, or sensitive environmentalist? Kind neighbor, or political manipulator? She sighed. Perhaps getting to know him and Sandy would shed some light on the mystery. And designing their gardens would be the perfect opportunity to do just that.

She turned the key and waited while the old engine chugged to life with a roar and clatter of ancient muffler. Best give it a minute to warm up, she thought, glancing across the lot. Street was standing beside his car, shoulders stooped, slowly shaking his head. "Something wrong?" she asked, pulling up beside him.

"The tires. They slashed the tires. I wouldn't have thought—"

"I'll call the police."

"Don't. There's no point in giving it any attention." He sighed. No longer cool and unflappable, he looked to Rachel like a lost little boy. "I didn't even consider turning on the alarm. It feels so safe here. Everything was going so well. . . ."

"Things like this aren't supposed to happen in Riverdale, Street. I'm so sorry." Tossing her collection of files and coffee cups from the passenger seat into the back of the Jeep, she ordered, "Get in. I'll drive you home."

Street obeyed, staring out the window at the crippled black car with an expression suggesting he'd just lost his best friend. "Is . . . is there a service station in town I can trust?"

Rachel touched his arm, an instinctive response to his obvious misery, and one she instantly regretted. *Hands off,* she warned herself. *Remember Sandy. Don't let those sad eyes tempt you.* "Don't worry, Street. The best mechanic in town married an old friend of mine. I'll call for you, if you like. He'll take very good care of your baby."

He grimaced. "Sorry. Guess I am taking it a bit too seriously. It's just that . . . you'd think I'd be used to it. Some of the projects we've backed in the past . . . well, we've seen our share of violence. But this—this feels like a personal attack, Rachel. I was starting to feel at home here."

"Don't let this shape your image of Riverdale, Street."

She pulled into his driveway. "There are lunatics every-where nowadays. Even here. Most of us are harmless, though. Who knows," she said with a wink, "once we get used to the idea, we might even start to like you."

Street grinned. "I hope so, Rachel. Come in for a minute, won't you? Sandy's probably making tea."

"Oh, I . . . I shouldn't."

"Please? You wouldn't leave me alone to break this news, would you? It's likely to send Sandy right around the bend. And anyway, you promised you'd call your friend about my 'baby,' remember?"

Obviously the man wouldn't take no for an answer. Rachel let herself be guided across the dark lawn.

"Sandy?" Street bellowed the name as he threw open the front door. "We've got company, Sandy. Get out here!"

Just when she was beginning to have some warm, neigh-borly feelings for Street, he managed to act like a braying jackass. Was he always so loud and abrupt with the poor woman? she wondered.

"Company? How lovely. I've just made some tea and biscuits."

Rachel spun to face the source of the oddly familiar voice, and gaped in stunned silence at the smiling face of Kit's beloved Bucky Buchanan.

A chorus of frogs, sheltered in the cattail fringe along the Mawr, trilled their serenade into the still night air. Rachel kept time with their music, matching the lazy swish-squeak of the porch swing to the rhythm of the riverbank song.

She sat curled into the corner of the old swing, gazing contentedly at the rockery. It was even more beautiful by moonlight, she thought, enjoying the moment and the sud-den rush of gratitude and affection she felt for Street. It was dangerous to entertain such feelings, but no longer for-bidden, now that she knew the truth about Sandy/Bucky.

She laughed, imagining the expression they must have

seen on her face when the little man met them at the door. She could almost feel Street's rich, deep laughter rumbling through her body, as it had while she stared in mute astonishment at Sandy Buchanan.

She remembered, too, Street's disarming smile, the laugh lines that crinkled the corners of his eyes when he'd leaned through the window of her Jeep to say good night. Almost close enough for a kiss. . . .

She shivered. His was a dangerous attraction, a powerful magnetism that drew her like a moth to a flame. Considering the moth's chances of survival, she warned herself to think about something else. Kit, for instance.

Over tea and biscuits in Street's kitchen, Bucky had told her that Kit talked of little else these days but the good times she shared with her new girlfriend. And he'd beamed with pleasure to learn from Rachel that Kit never tired of regaling her with stories about "my Bucky" and "my brother, Bobby."

When she'd wondered aloud whether she'd ever meet the wonderful Bobby, Bucky and Street had exchanged cryptic glances. "Very soon, I should think," said Bucky. "Yes," added Street. "He's quite a character. I'm sure you'll like him."

What kind of man must Bobby be? she wondered. Admired by three people as vastly different as Kit, Sandy, and Street? She could hardly wait to find out.

Chapter Eleven

Approaching the long row of stone buildings at the east end of Main Street, Rachel slowed the old Jeep to a crawl. If Street's Porsche was parked in the driveway, she would keep right on going. Avoid temptation.

She craned her neck to see around the horribly over-grown hedge of Chinese elm that hid his house from the street. Good. No sign of the shiny black car. Sandy Buchanan's silver-gray BMW stood alone in the driveway, prim and fastidious like its owner.

Rachel pulled in beside it, careful to leave plenty of room for the Porsche, on the off chance that Street might return before she'd finished. Quickly banishing the hopeful thought that he might, indeed, do just that, she pushed the door open and sat for a moment, surveying the front yard.

She had stopped by, at Mr. Buchanan's insistence, after dinner last Wednesday evening, to discuss their plans for the garden. Now came the fun part, making it all work.

Just a few feet away, the front door flew open with a loud bang, disgorging an aproned Sandy Buchanan, who scurried toward her wearing an enormous grin on his flour-dusted face.

"Rachel! How lovely to see you! Welcome back!"

"Thanks, Mr. Buchanan."

"Oh, please, call me Sandy. Everyone does. Except our little Kit, of course."

"Sandy it is, then. I won't disturb you; just wanted to walk the gardens in the sunlight. I need to take some measurements, maybe make some sketches, if that's all right with you."

"Oh, absolutely. Wonderful! Get rid of this horrid jungle, won't you, Rachel? The sooner, the better."

She laughed. "Don't worry, Sandy. It's a beautiful property. With a little planning and hard work, you won't recognize the place. You'll love it."

"Come have some tea, dear. And zucchini bread. It's hot from the oven. Mmm."

"Oh, I—I really shouldn't . . ." *Stick to business,* she reminded herself. But poor Sandy looked so disappointed.

"Oh, well." He sighed. "I've been stuck talking to myself all day. A little company would be such a treat, but . . ." He sighed again, rolling his eyes skyward and making her feel horribly mean.

"Okay, okay. No more guilt . . . please. You and your zucchini bread are pretty hard to resist. Let me look around out back first, get the feel of the place. Then I'll join you." She smiled to see his obvious pleasure at her change of heart.

"Just come right in when you're finished, dear. I'll be in the kitchen."

Wandering leisurely through Street's backyard and along the riverbank, Rachel was charmed by the peaceful setting. Vivid images of its eventual transformation crowded her mind as she carefully measured distances and scribbled notes on important features and interesting plants. This would someday be a very special place, she thought, anxious to begin her sketches and see the project under way.

"Sandy?" Pushing open the kitchen door, she peered inside to find the little man perched high on a chair in the far corner. He was rummaging through a cupboard and emitting a seemingly endless string of "tsk-tsk-tsks."

"Lose something?" she asked, dropping her backpack beside the table as he sprang to the floor.

Sandy's face blanched. "There's no tarragon!" He moaned in obvious distress.

Rachel's hand flew to her mouth, barely in time to prevent the laugh that had threatened to erupt. Was he serious? "Tarragon?" She was unable to say more for fear of giggling at him.

"Dinner will be ruined. I'm at my wits' end." Sandy ripped the apron from around his waist and wiped his hands as he hurried toward her. "Please, Rachel, do sit down. I've cleared the table for you. Isn't it just the perfect place to sketch the garden? You can see the whole thing from this window."

She nodded, sinking into the offered chair.

"You look warm. Would you like some iced tea, or shall I put the kettle on?"

"Iced tea would be perfect, Sandy, thanks."

He bustled around the room, returning seconds later with a frosty glass of tea and a plate of still-warm zucchini bread.

Rachel took one sip of the lemony-sweet liquid. It was the best she'd ever tasted. "Sandy! This is wonderful. I've never had anything quite so delicious."

He blushed, nodding as if to agree with her assessment. "None of that powdered stuff in this household. Made it myself this morning. Steeped in the sun, that's the secret. Try the bread."

"Mmmmm. Oh, Sandy. It's incredible! Where did you find this recipe?"

"That's a deep, dark secret, Rachel, my dear. But I'm

90

so glad you like it. I'll give you some to take home."
Sandy glanced anxiously at his watch. "Forgive me, dear,
but I really must run to the store. Tarragon. Dinner. The
quality of food. You understand. Please, make yourself at
home. I shan't be long."

He was out the door before Rachel could protest, leaving
her to shake her head at his lovable eccentricity. Reaching
into her backpack, she retrieved her favorite mechanical
pencil and a roll of tracing paper, spreading a generous
length across the table. She stared out the window, seeking
inspiration as she nibbled on another morsel of Sandy's
top-secret zucchini bread.

The kitchen smelled of cinnamon and spices, comfortable and homey. She found herself wickedly tempted to ex-
plore the rest of the house. Two visits to the Wellman
sanctum and she still had absolutely no idea what lay beyond the kitchen. What could it hurt? she thought, savoring
another gulp of tea. Just a harmless little reward for giving
up her Saturday afternoon to work on Street's site plans. If
Sandy came back unexpectedly, she could always say she
was looking for the bathroom.

She wandered down the long hall and into the living
room, pleasantly surprised by the elegantly understated de-
cor. Masculine with lots of earthy colors and rich textures.
Subtle. Tasteful.

A beautifully framed print hung on the far wall, whistling
swans in flight, and she tiptoed the length of the room to
examine it more closely. Bateman. Just as she'd thought.
And not a print. This was the real thing, the original.
"Rachel, honey," she whispered, "you're so far out of
your league, you're not even in the ballpark."

She peeked nervously out the front window. The coast
was still clear. Did she dare venture upstairs? Oh, why not?
She'd suffer untold feelings of guilt over this blatant tres-
pass anyway. She might as well make it worthwhile. With
a last glance out the window, she darted up the staircase.

Street's room was first left at the top of the stairs. No

sign on the door announced it, but Rachel was certain. She could almost feel his presence. Stepping through the door, she was met by the wonderful, musky sandalwood-and-leather scent of him that seemed to stay with her for hours each time they met. She breathed deeply.

Stop! Her eyes flew open. She'd been leaning against the doorjamb, her arms, imagined as his, wrapped tightly around her. Horrified by her own emotions, she turned and ran, not stopping until she reached the kitchen.

Sheepishly glancing around the room, half expecting to be caught at her escapade, she breathed a sigh of relief to find herself still alone. She sank into the chair, grabbing her pencil and tearing into her work, fighting to close her mind to thoughts of Street, to ignore the scent of him that lingered in her nostrils. She forced herself to concentrate on the scene beyond the window, and on the garden growing slowly on the page.

Street withdrew to the shadows of the hallway, hoping to linger unseen for just a while longer. Rachel's presence certainly explained Sandy's cryptic message on the car phone, and his conspicuous absence now. The man was an incorrigible matchmaker.

He watched, intrigued, as the tracing paper she'd spread across his kitchen table came slowly alive with the forms of his soon-to-be garden. Vague shapes for the time being, but even from so far across the room he felt pleasure at the direction her imagination was taking. She had listened well, he thought, had understood his needs and Sandy's demands, and seemed to have a natural talent for design.

Her considerable other "talents" didn't escape his admiration either, treated as he was to such a splendid view, enhanced by the long rays of afternoon sunshine that streamed through the window. Rachel seemed completely at ease, comfortably at home in his house, totally engrossed in her sketches, and unaware of the eyes that caressed her from afar. She had abandoned her sandals under the table, and sat with one leg curled gracefully beneath her, the other twined around the chair leg. She wore faded blue jeans, and a long linen shirt.

The pencil suddenly dropped from her fingers, rolling unnoticed onto the floor, as Rachel lowered her head into her hands, wearily massaging her temples and then the back of her neck. Street leaned heavily against the doorjamb, wishing those were his hands, lost in that tangle of reddish-blond curls. The memory of that night in her kitchen, her warm skin beneath his fingers, the sudden prickling tremor that telegraphed her response, were still vivid, still able to wake him in the night. Tempting. He sighed. The attraction he'd felt for her, almost from their first meeting, was becoming far too powerful to ignore.

Moaning a barely audible little sigh, Rachel rolled her head from side to side, then raised her arms in a decidedly feline stretch, stopping to twist her hair into a knot that somehow clung, unaided, to the nape of her neck. She rolled her head again.

"I can cure that for you," he said, stepping out of the shadows. She jumped, startled by his sudden appearance, then smiled up at him with a pleasantly questioning arch of her eyebrows.

"Trust me," he murmured, resting strong, confident hands on her shoulders as he moved to stand behind her.

Street began to knead, his thumbs tracing ever-deepening circles, and Rachel gripped the edge of the table, certain she'd scream if he didn't stop.

"Relax," he commanded, driving his thumbs into tightly knotted bundles of muscle and nerve.

"Ohhh . . . owww . . . nooo!" Trying to pull away, she only succeeded in tightening his hold. "Relax? While you torture me? How do I manage that?" She writhed beneath him, struggling to escape the touch that only moments ago she'd fantasized might hold such possibilities, the possibility of intense pain not among them.

"Trust me, Rachel." He leaned down to breathe the

words into her ear, still laboring over her taut muscles. "Relax."

Trust him? Forcing herself to release her viselike grip on the table, to let her arms hang limply at her sides and her head loll, took every bit of her strength and concentration. Anything to make him stop. At the very moment of absolute certainty that she could bear it no longer, he did stop. And to her utter amazement the tension, the looming threat of headache, was gone. Street's fingers lingered on the bare skin of her neck, artfully banishing any remnants of pain.

Rachel inhaled deeply, holding her breath in, unwilling to let herself respond to Street's touch in all the ways she seemed so very determined to try.

"Better?" He spoke the word close to her ear again, so close she imagined she could feel his lips brush the skin on her neck. Dry. And hot.

Maybe she hadn't imagined it. Street had taken both her hands in his and was pulling her to her feet, drawing her toward him until she stood too close, a mere hair's breadth from his broad expanse of chest.

"Much better," she whispered, with a smile she sincerely hoped would not betray the confusion she felt. A fire, too long cold, had begun to glow within her, and Rachel felt her heart pound as she looked up into his sparkling gray eyes. Alight with passion, they seemed ready to consume her.

Street spun toward the living room, still holding one of Rachel's hands tightly in his own. "Come," he said. "We'll finish the cure."

Rachel wanted to stay in the familiar, brightly lit safety of the kitchen. More than that, she wanted to run away. As far away from this man as her suddenly weak legs would carry her. But Street held fast to her hand, pulled her through the doorway, and her traitorous feet meekly followed where he led.

She felt her heart begin to race, heard its rapid, pounding

rhythm in her ears. He guided her across the living room, carefully settling her in what had to be the most comfortable chair she'd ever experienced. It reclined in response to one touch of his finger.

Unsure of her emotions, she tried to avoid thinking about them, examining the chair instead. She ran her hands appreciatively along the armrests. The leather felt buttery soft and warm.

Street sat on the matching footstool, once again admonishing her to relax as he lifted her bare feet into his lap. She clenched her fists, ready to bear the pain as his long fingers slowly began to massage her right instep. This time, though, his hands were incredibly gentle, working in tiny circles, out toward her toes, then massaging each one in turn. She closed her eyes, convinced that the man had a magic touch, and afraid she was powerless to resist his spell.

When he finished, resting her feet on the stool as he stood, she opened her eyes to smile up at him, so relaxed, she almost felt drugged. "What did you just do? And where did you learn it?"

Street laughed. "That was my best attempt at 'the cure.' Something Sandy taught me. I have no idea where he picked it up. He says it's his own secret brand of reflexology. Whatever it is, it works."

"Mmmmm." Rachel let her eyes drift closed. "Sure does."

"Just rest awhile; I'll be right back."

The room fell silent except for the slow and steady sound of her own breathing. She stayed perfectly still, reluctant to interrupt the rather remarkable sensations that continued to course through her body like some tingling, electrical current. *Magic,* she thought again, and opened her eyes to watch a somehow larger-than-life Street Wellman stride toward her across the room.

Another touch of his finger and the chair glided upright, returning Rachel to the real world. She tucked both feet beneath her, curling into the chair and freeing the footstool for Street. He sat, offering a steaming mug of tea. "It's very hot. Careful you don't burn your tongue."

A pungent, spicy aroma rose in a cloud from the mug. "Mmmmm," she said again, letting her eyes fall momentarily shut. It was amazing how relaxed she'd become.

"You look tired, Rachel." Street's voice was heavy with concern. "The garden plans can wait, you know. You *are* entitled to a day off."

Rachel shook her head, withdrawing her hand and quickly averting her eyes from his intense scrutiny. "This is very . . . unusual. What is it?" she asked, gingerly sipping the hot tea.

"Another of Sandy's secrets, I'm afraid. But I'm sure he'd be glad to give you some. Don't avoid the subject, Rachel. I'm worried about you."

"Don't be. I'm fine." She forced a smile, glancing briefly in Street's direction. He wasn't smiling back.

"I don't think I've ever seen you off duty. Ten-hour days at the office, then home to take care of that huge property all by yourself. Not to mention the long hours you put in at Riverdale Place. Where's the time for *you*?"

"I have to keep busy," she said, cringing at the sound of those words. Where had that come from? "I *like* to keep busy" would have put an end to the worrisome conversation, but that needful word had slipped out. That painful truth. Since Peter's death, she kept busy to stay sane. Free time had become a dangerous commodity. If she let Street continue to chip away at the protective shell she'd built around her emotions, there'd be more at stake than just an annoying physical attraction. *The man's a client,* she told herself again. *Don't let him in.* But in her heart, Rachel. knew they'd both already crossed the line.

"How did Peter die, Rachel? An accident?"

She heard herself gasp, felt the blood drain from her face and tears sting her eyes. Watching Street's anguished reaction, she blinked them away, gulping one deep breath after another in a desperate attempt to compose herself. Street sheltered her hand with his and this time she didn't pull away.

"Rachel, I'm sorry," he whispered. "I'm so sorry."

"No. It's okay. You just surprised me, that's all. Reading me so well. Peter could do that, too."

She tried to smile, not quite succeeding. "It wasn't an accident. He . . . he was very ill. I'm sorry. It's still hard for me to talk about it. He just went downhill so fast, as if . . . as if he'd grown old overnight. I tried, but at the end, I just couldn't take care of him. That's when he went to Riverdale Place. I owe them a lot, Street. Things money can't buy. That's why I give my time."

She stood, separating herself from the reassuring comfort of Street's hand. "I should be there now," she said, glancing at her watch. "Please tell Sandy how much I enjoyed the zucchini bread."

"Rachel?"

She backed away before he could touch her again with those magic hands. His eyes had warned her. He'd been about to wrap those strong arms around her, hold her close, comfort her. She could not let that happen.

Street caught up with her in the kitchen, watching in silence as she gathered the tracing paper into a tight roll, then swept her pencil and notebook into her backpack.

"Rachel?" He stood between her and the door. "Why are you running away from me? I don't bite. I'd never hurt you."

"Please, Street. I need to go. *Now*."

Street held her for one long moment in a gaze she could not escape, then stepped slowly aside, swinging open the door.

Chapter Twelve

"What is this place, Bobby? Are those magic rocks?" Wide-eyed, Kit pointed to an outcropping at the side of the road where a single tree seemed to grow, as if by magic, from a narrow crack in the limestone.

"Might be, sweetheart. It's called the quarry, and I've certainly seen a lot of wonders here." He smiled, remembering the "wonders" of lovely Rachel as she made her swift retreat from the lake after their first almost-meeting.

Rounding the last bend in the road, he wheeled the Porsche to a stop under the lone tree, and smiled again.

"Look, Bobby, it's Rachel's car." Kit bounced happily in her seat. "She's here! She's here! Let's go find her!"

"Good idea, Kitten, but let's surprise her. Can you be quiet as a mouse? We'll pretend we're playing hide and seek, okay?"

"I can be *really* quiet, Bobby," she said, in a very loud whisper. "I promise. Where should we look?"

Hand in hand they made their way to the lakeshore.

"There. There she is, Bobby. Can we yell 'surprise' now?"

"No, wait. I've got a much better idea. You found her first, Kitten. You should be the one to surprise her."

"D'you think she's asleep, Bobby? She's awfully quiet."

"Looks like it. Now, why don't you . . ." Street bent to whisper in her ear.

Kit jumped with glee, clapping both hands over her mouth to hold back a giggle. "But if she gets mad, I'm telling it was your idea."

Sinking onto the rocky beach, Street watched as his sister crept slowly along the shore toward the slumbering Rachel. Scooping a double handful of water from the lake, she turned with a whoop and sent a frigid shower raining down onto Rachel's sun-baked skin.

"Aaaahhhh!" Rachel shot bolt upright in a single motion, gasping for breath as the shock of cold water wore off. "What the . . . ? Kit? How on earth . . . ?"

"We fooled you, Rachel! Ha-ha on you!"

"What . . . ? We?" Rachel grabbed for her towel and wrestled with the top of her bathing suit, quickly shrugging the straps back over her shoulders. "Who's with you, Kit? How did you get here?"

"With Bobby. We came for the turtles. There's real, live turtles here, Rachel, and I'm gonna find them. Bobby told me. See?"

Rachel squinted into the sun, following Kit's gaze. *Oh my gosh! Bobby looked so much like . . . oh my gosh!*

Hands shoved deep into the pockets of his jeans, Street sauntered along the shore, coming to a stop just inches from her blanket, his broad shoulders blocking the sun. "Catching flies, Rachel?"

Oh, my gosh! Rachel tried to close her mouth, with little success. This was just too much. *Too much.* She tugged nervously at her bathing suit as Street dropped onto the blanket beside her.

"Allow me to introduce myself. I'm Kit's big brother, Bobby, and I'm very pleased to meet you at last. Kitten's told me so much about you.'' He held out his hand and smiled again.

Rachel stared at him, at the crooked smile, the mischievous twinkle in his gray eyes. *Street and Bobby? One and the same?*

''It's customary to say hello, or something to that effect, when you meet somebody, Rachel.'' She felt his elbow nudge her arm.

''It's Bobby, Rachel. What's the matter? Don't you like him?'' Kit knelt to give her a hug. ''You're not mad at me, are you? For the water, I mean?'' She jumped up, planting her hands on her hips. ''It was Bobby's idea. He told me to. Honest!''

''Oh, really? Your idea, was it, *Bobby*?'' Pulling Kit down onto the blanket again, Rachel smiled. ''Of course I'm not mad at you, sweetie. You really got me a good one, that's for sure.'' She hugged the girl warmly, releasing her to scamper down the beach, then turned to Street. ''You, on the other hand . . . why have you kept this from me all these weeks? You and Sandy? And who else? What's the big secret, *Bobby*?''

''I—I'm sorry, Rachel. It's not that I meant to deceive you.'' He chuckled. ''As a matter of fact, Sandy played the same game with me. I had no idea that my Rachel Jennings-Porter, landscape architect extraordinaire, was the same lovely lady he'd met at Riverdale Place, the one my sister took such an instant liking to.'' He touched her arm, running one finger lightly down the inside of her wrist. ''Forgive me. I wanted to tell you, but the time was never right, and we have to be careful, for Kit's sake. There've been problems—people who've taken advantage, even a kidnap threat, once.''

''Oh, no!''

He nodded. ''That's why she's not living at home. I just can't be there around the clock to keep her safe. And that's why she's known as Kit Laurence—our mother's name.'' He took a deep breath and glanced protectively at Kit who

100

was gleefully tossing stones into the lake. "So far, only Rina and Dr. Hughson know who she really is . . . and they're sworn to secrecy. Nobody needs to know she's related to big, bad Street Wellman."

It was true, thought Rachel, feeling a surge of compassion for the man. All the money in the world couldn't buy happiness. "Don't talk about yourself that way, Street. You're the best brother in the world, as far as Kit's concerned. And she's got me convinced, too." She smiled up at him. "Your little sister's a very special person. Her friendship means a great deal to me. It's not just part of the job."

"Bobby, Rachel. Look at what I found!" Kit bounced happily along the rocky shore, laughing and pointing excitedly into the water.

"What, Kit? I can't see what you're looking at." Rachel scrambled to her feet, momentarily oblivious to the fact that her bathing suit left very little to the imagination, and ran to Kit's side. "What did you find?"

"Take a mental cold shower," muttered Street. *"Start now."*

"Did you say something, Street?"

"Er . . . cold water. I'm staying here."

"But, Bobby, I want a picture of the turtle. It . . . it's . . . aawwww! Where'd it go?" Kit's lower lip began to tremble. Rachel suspected her turtle "find" had been nothing more than a rock brought to life by the rippling water.

"Hey, it's okay. Maybe the turtle swam away. I'll bet he's playing hide-and-seek with us."

"Maybe . . ." Kit looked thoughtful. "But we can find him later, okay, Rachel? I'm hungry!"

"Me, too. Did you bring lunch?"

"Yup. Bucky made it. He makes the best picnics."

"Mmmmm, I bet he does. Let's eat. Then I'll show you where my favorite old turtle takes his sunbath in the afternoon."

"Bobby? Bobby, are you hungry? We wanna eat, okay?

101

Please?'' Kit bounced up the beach, landing with a thud on the recumbent form of her brother, who had lazily draped one hand over his eyes as he lounged in the sun.

"*Oooof!* Ow. I'm killed."

Kit giggled. "Sorry, Bobby. Are you hungry?"

Without moving a muscle, he answered, "Yes, Kit, I could definitely eat now. Only thing is, *someone* is going to have to go to the car for Sandy's picnic basket." He sighed. "Guess that'd be me." Slowly he let his arm slide away from his eyes and rolled onto his side, tumbling Kit onto the sand. He examined Rachel from tip to toe, wearing what she thought was a decidedly wicked-looking grin.

"Hungry, Rachel?"

She blushed. Time to cover up. Actually it was way past time to cover up, judging from the way Street was devouring her with his eyes. She hastily pulled on her shirt, leaving it unbuttoned, knotting the shirttails across her midriff. Then she tied her wraparound skirt firmly around her waist. Street, she thought, looked more than a little disappointed.

"Very hungry," she said, reaching for her beach bag. "And somewhere in here is my lunch. A cheese-and-pickle sandwich. I'd be happy to share, if you don't feel like walking back to the car."

Kit tugged on Rachel's arm, almost toppling her off balance. "Cheese and pickle? Yucky! Bucky made all yummy stuff for us. I don't think I want cheese and pickle." She turned a vaguely worried look on Rachel who, as usual, melted completely.

"I was just kidding, Kit. You should try a bite of mine, though. You just might like it. *I* do."

"Well, if you ladies will excuse me," said Street, hauling himself up from the blanket, "I'll just head up to the car and get our lunch right now. And I think I'll take you up on that offer, Rachel."

"Offer? What . . . ?"

"To try a bite of yours. I might like it." Street winked.

"Cheese and pickle, I mean." With an outrageous bow and flourish, he turned and jogged effortlessly down the beach.

Forcing herself to look at Kit, rather than at the perfectly proportioned retreating form of Street Wellman, extraordinary brother and all-around gorgeous guy, Rachel suggested they take a walk along the shore. "Old Man Turtle likes to take his nap in a tucked-away spot just over there."

Taking Kit's arm, she steered her toward the spot where she'd last seen the old fellow, the day of her fateful first encounter with Street. *Keep your mind on the turtles!* she warned herself, as Kit skipped into the lead.

"Oh, Rachel, look! I think I see him!" Kit's voice squeaked with delight, and Rachel breathed a sigh of relief. It seemed, however, that Kit was not destined to see the old man today, or any other real turtles, for that matter. More than likely, all her splashing around in the water had sent any and all self-respecting wildlife hightailing it for cover.

Kit's lower lip was trembling again, and Rachel was glad to be able to offer the distraction of "Here comes your brother with the picnic basket."

Kit brightened visibly at the mention of her brother, and pulled away from Rachel, running along the beach, jumping over small stones in happy abandon. Her dismay of seconds ago was long forgotten, but Rachel was learning how quickly Kit's moods could change. Looking out for her was a big job. She wondered how Street managed to keep everything together, and how it had come to be his responsibility. He was a pretty amazing man, she thought, admiring him as he deposited Sandy's picnic basket on the corner of her blanket. *Now cut that out!*

"Hey, how about some help with this?" he grumbled.

Kit knelt to peer into the basket and squealed with delight. "Look! Bucky made tuna and watercress sandwiches for me, roast beef and hot mustard for Bobby, and there's two big pieces of chocolate cake for dessert." She glanced up at Rachel. "Uh . . . there's lots of salad and

some deviled eggs, too, if you like that stuff.'' Her disgusted expression spoke volumes about her feelings on
"salad and deviled eggs and stuff,'' and both Rachel and
Street burst out laughing.

Kit was indignant. "I don't think it's so funny. All that
stuff is for grownups. I hate it.'' She began pulling con-
tainers from the basket.

Street and Rachel exchanged looks. For grownups?
Every once in a while, it became painfully obvious that Kit
was very much a child. Street cleared his throat and
abruptly looked away. "Let me help you with that, Kit.''

His voice sounded huskier than usual. How hard it must
be for him. Every single day of his life. Rachel watched as
he opened the last container and placed it on the blanket.
"Ladies, lunch is served. Shall we?''

Bucky had outdone himself, as usual. In addition to sandwiches, there were two kinds of pâté, soft, fresh bread, and
crisp, exotic crackers. There were three cheeses and five
different kinds of pickles, carrot and celery sticks, broccoli
and cauliflower pieces, and two kinds of dip. Bottles of
fruit juice and spring water completed the feast. For a few
seconds, the three just stood and stared at it. Then common
sense, and hunger, took over. Rachel left her humble
cheese-and-pickle sandwich in her bag.

Much later, after Kit had pronounced herself "stuffed''
and then gone back for more, after Street had insisted that
Rachel have his piece of chocolate cake and they'd ended
up splitting it, after eating so much that the blanket resem-
bled the site of some great historical food fight, Kit pushed
herself up to wander the beach again, eyes peeled for those
pesky, hiding turtles. She'd taken a short nap, about five
minutes in length, after her last declaration that she was
stuffed, and now she was raring to go again.

Turning lazily to Street, Rachel asked quietly, "Will she
always be this way, do you think?''

"What way? Full of life and love and fun, bringing joy
into everyone's life? Or do you mean, will she ever grow

104

up?'' His face became a study in thoughtfulness and he continued before Rachel could respond. ''I don't know what will happen, Rachel. But they tell us, most likely, she'll be the way she is now for the rest of her life.'' He paused. ''We're . . . used to it, Sandy and I. And we're all the family there is left.''

He seemed so wistful, so almost-sad. There was no way she could sit quietly by and not say a word to help him.

''Street, what happened to Kit? And your parents? Do you feel like talking about it?'' She held her breath. Would he take offense? Think she was prying?

He turned slowly, looking into her eyes, the slight mistiness of a moment ago clearing as he let down his guard and opened up to her for the first time. ''Oh, Rachel, it all seems so long ago. It's almost like a dream . . . a nightmare. With Kit, I—''

Street cleared his throat, but couldn't ease the catch in his voice. ''Kit and I were fishing, out on the lake behind our house. It was a beautiful, spring morning—early May. The air was warm, but the water in the lake was still icy.'' He gave a small, lopsided smile that tugged mightily at Rachel's heart. ''We used to fish there all the time. She always caught more fish than I did, just seemed to have the magic touch. . . .''

Rachel leaned close and touched his arm. ''Are you all right?''

''What? Oh, yeah, I'm fine, really. I don't mind telling you. If it helps you to look after Kit . . . Anyway, we'd been out for a couple of hours, and we stopped to eat lunch.'' He chuckled. ''Even then, Sandy would always do his best to stuff us to oblivion at every opportunity. So, we were eating, and joking around . . . Kit still had her line in the water; she always did that, just pressed the rod between her knee and the side of the boat. I remember we were about to start on dessert when she got a bite—a good one. A good one,'' he repeated, shaking his head.

''Well, she dropped her food, and grabbed for her rod.

105

It happened so fast, you know? But I always see it in slow motion, over and over.'' His voice shook. ''Her knee slipped against the side of the boat. She fell. She was still hanging on to that rod for dear life. I—I couldn't help her. She was scrambling around, trying to get onto her knees, grappling with the rod . . . then she leaned over to see what she'd hooked. Something big, she said. She was all excited. Before I could yell at her to wait, she fell over the side. She still had the rod in her hand.'' He drew a ragged breath and passed a hand across his eyes. Then he turned to look directly at Rachel again. ''I—I jumped right in after her, not even a second later. She was always a good swimmer, she should've been fine, but I just knew something was wrong . . . so wrong. She got . . . she was . . . her line was snarled on something, it got wrapped around her ankle, and she . . . she couldn't get hold of the boat. Her head was under water. She was panicking, screaming for help.''

''Oh, Street.'' Rachel could see it. Every word a vivid picture in her mind. Terrifying. What must it be like for him?

''I dove, started to untangle her, but I—I had to come up for air a couple of times . . . *I had to.* The water was so cold. By the time I got her free and into the boat, she was unconscious. I gave her mouth-to-mouth, and I remember screaming for somebody to help me, but nobody could hear. I got her to the house as fast as I could. They said there was nothing more I could have done. . . .'' He made a soft choking sound, as if he couldn't go on. But he did. ''She was in a coma for three days. I never left her, even though Mom and Dad tried to drag me away. I prayed that she'd live. I *begged* her to live, told her we'd always do things together. She finally woke up . . . the way she is now. And she's never changed. Except—''

He frowned, still lost in his memories. ''Except when our parents died. It was—it was a plane crash. She didn't understand, disappeared inside herself then . . . for months. Sandy and I were afraid she'd never come back.'' He

106

straightened himself involuntarily, as if to make himself strong. "But she did, mostly thanks to Sandy. He really is quite an amazing person."

Street winked, obviously beginning to feel a bit better. "Guess I don't have to tell you how great he is. And he thinks the world of you, by the way."

Rachel swiped a hand across her eyes. She wouldn't cry, wouldn't cause him any more pain. Not if she could help it. She looked across the beach at Kit, as much to hide her emotional upset, as to see what the girl was up to. She never wandered too far, always checking to make sure her big brother was still nearby.

"Rachel?"

She brushed at her eyes again as Street cupped her chin in his hand. "Thank you for listening."

She let his strong fingers pull her close, lifting her mouth until she was almost close enough to feel the warmth of his breath on her face. "Street, I'm so sorry," she murmured, half-closing her eyes against the sun, or was it against the heat of his touch? "I had no idea."

He dropped his hand and leaned back, regarding her thoughtfully as he relaxed onto one elbow. "It's okay, really. I guess I just felt I had to tell you, to share something of my life with you. Anything to let you see that I am not the kind of monster you seem to think I am. Well, sometimes, anyway."

That blush again! It was as if the man could read her mind. "Aw, Street, that's not the way it is. It's just that I get a little . . . a little . . ." What on earth was she trying to say?

"A little confused, maybe?" he asked. "A little lonely? Lost? I feel that way, too. A lot of the time."

"I—I . . ." *What?* What was it she wanted to say? She was strangely tongue-tied, certain she'd end up embarrassing herself. And him as well, most likely. It was time to change the subject. "I think we'd better see what Kit's up to. Don't you? She seems awfully quiet all of a sudden."

107

"What's the matter, sweetie?" she called. "Are you ready to go home?"

Kit trudged up the beach and flopped onto the blanket, turning soulful eyes on Rachel. "I can't find any turtles. And Bobby promised I'd see some. He said there's lots here."

Uh-oh, mood swing alert! Do something! "Hey, I've got an idea! I have a whole collection of glass animals at my house, with five turtles that you've never seen. How'd you like to come back and take a look at them with me?"

Street's face creased with uncertainty. "I don't know, Rachel. Kit should really be getting back to Riverdale Place for supper."

"Oh, please, Bobby! Can't we have dinner at Rachel's? Spaghetti? Please? It's my very favorite. Bucky makes it for me whenever I want."

"Now, wait just a minute," said Street. "You can't impose on Rachel like that."

Kit snuggled a little closer. "Can Bobby come, too, Rachel? *Please . . . ?*"

Chapter Thirteen

"My animals all live on a shelf in the bedroom, Kit. Not quite as fancy as your beautiful glass case, but I think you'll like it. C'mon up!"

Rachel dropped her beach bag on the hall floor and bounded up the stairs with Kit in hot pursuit.

"Wait!" Kit stopped short, tugging on Rachel's sleeve to make sure she didn't get too far ahead. "Bobby, don't just stand there, silly. Come see Rachel's room. We're waiting."

Street looked as close to embarrassed as Rachel had ever seen him. Shrugging helplessly, he shoved his hands deep into the pockets of his jeans before he answered. "You, um . . . you just go along with Rachel, Kitten. I'll wait here."

"Why?" Kit's lower lip fell into an instant pout. "I thought you wanted to see the turtles, too."

"It's just . . . it's not polite for a gentleman to go barging into a lady's bedroom uninvited, Kit. That's why. Now go. And stop your pouting."

"But, Bobby, she did invite us, didn't you Rachel?" Kit glanced hopefully up at her, begging reassurance.

"Of course I did, sweetie. And you're more than welcome to join us, Street. In fact, I'll give you both the grand tour."

Street shrugged again, flashing her a charming grin, and then trudged up the stairs behind them. *Anything for little sister,* she thought, suddenly remembering her own uninvited prowl around his house, his bedroom. She wondered what he'd think if he knew.

Rounding the corner, Rachel breathed a sigh of relief. She'd remembered to make the bed. The room looked quite presentable. No lingerie strewn around the floor, or anything. "This is it. Small, but cozy. What d'you think, Kit?"

"Ohhh, Rachel. It's sooo pretty! Isn't it pretty, Bobby? Kit's eyes shone with delight as she bounced across the room and onto the four-poster bed. "Can I have lacy curtains like those for my room, Bobby? Please?"

Rachel laughed. "I made them, Kit. Maybe we could go shopping for some fabric and make a set for you. Would you like that?"

"I sure would. Oh, Rachel! You're the best friend I ever had. Next to Bobby and Bucky, I mean. The very best. And—"

Rachel's little menagerie caught Kit's eye mid-sentence, and all else was forgotten. "Oh, look! They're so cute. Bobby, look. There's a giraffe, and an elephant—two elephants. And dogs, and kittens." Kit giggled with delight. "And look at the turtles!" She touched each tiny figurine in turn, blissfully naming every animal as she oohed and aahed her approval. The turtles, of course, were her favorites.

Rachel sank onto the end of her bed, delighted by Kit's response to her little collection, and utterly enchanted by the expression of tenderness and love on Street's face as he watched his sister at play. He sighed, turning to smile warmly at her, mouthing a silent "Thank you."

Momentarily lost in each other's eyes, Street and Rachel jumped in unison when Kit's voice rang out, quite unexpectedly, behind them.

"I know what this is, Rachel. Bobby and Bucky have one in their new kitchen. It's a message machine, isn't it? I know. People can talk to it when they phone and you're not home. And look! Your red light's blinking. That means somebody phoned you."

Kit jabbed a finger at the PLAY button, proudly announcing, "I know how these things work, see? I wonder who phoned you?" Throwing herself across the bed beside Rachel, arms and legs akimbo, Kit listened with rapt attention as Danny Minelli's mellow tenor filled the room.

"Hi there, beautiful. How's the most beautiful landscape architect I know?"

Rachel felt the blush overtake her as she struggled to escape Kit's impulsive bear hug. She had to stop the tape. There was no telling what Danny might say next.

"I just got home," the voice crooned. "Hot day, isn't it? I'm standing here thinking about you. Thinking about a shower. Thinking about a *cold* shower . . ."

Street lounged against the doorjamb, arms folded, gray eyes laughing, as Rachel struggled to break free of Kit's grasp and lunged for the STOP button, cursing Danny Minelli under her breath.

"Who was that? Is he your boyfriend? I like him. He's funny." Rolling onto her back, Kit let her head hang over the edge of the bed and stared up at Rachel, upside-down and slightly cross-eyed. "Why's your face so red? Did you get sunburned today?"

The belly laugh Street had struggled so hard to contain suddenly erupted.

"That's enough!" Rachel flashed a warning with blue eyes turned suddenly icy.

But Street couldn't stop. He held his sides and laughed until they ached, oblivious to Kit's astonishment and Rachel's glacial stare.

"Are you quite finished?"

Uh-oh. The lady was not amused.

"Because, really, I don't see what's so terribly funny." Turning her back, Rachel hauled Kit to her feet and said sweetly, "No, Kit, Danny's not my boyfriend. Just a friend. An old friend who ought to know better than to leave messages like *that* on my answering machine. I'll deal with him later."

"Why'd he have to tell you about his shower, Rachel? Did he want you to wash his back, or something?" Kit twisted both arms behind her. "Sometimes it's hard to reach, you know?" She squirmed awkwardly in her attempt to prove that Danny might, indeed, need some help to wash his back.

Rachel smiled in spite of herself. It was definitely time to change the subject. "I know what you mean, Kit. But I'm sure Danny will manage just fine on his own. What do you say we check out the kitchen? I could use some help with our spaghetti dinner."

"Yeah! I'm hungry!" Kit skipped down the hall, stopping abruptly on the top step with a dramatic roll of her eyes. "Bucky says I mustn't run on the stairs. He says it's not ladylike." Sighing, as if being ladylike was a fate worse than death, Kit dropped one delicate hand on the banister and strode elegantly, and very slowly, down the steps. Once at the bottom, she rounded the corner at full speed and made a beeline for the kitchen.

It felt good to have people in the house. And laughter. She'd been sad and alone far too long. And Danny was right about one thing. Peter had wanted her to get on with life.

While she set the table for three, Street and Kit stood side by side at the kitchen sink, tearing lettuce into a bowl, cleaning celery and radishes, and slicing tomatoes for their salad. Kit had insisted that nobody else could do a proper job. "Bucky taught me how. And even if all this crunchy green stuff is totally yucky-gross, it's good for us. And Bucky says I make it the best." Well, who could argue with that?

Kit had stopped working and now stood, head bowed, as if confused about what she should do next. "Would you two like a little help?" asked Rachel, stepping up to the sink and slipping an arm around Kit's wisp of a waist.

The stalk of celery Kit had been washing slipped from her hand into the sink as she turned to look at Rachel.

"What's wrong, sweetie?" She instinctively tightened her hold. "Kit?" Something was very wrong. *"Street!"*

A faint tremor ran through Kit's slim body. The blush of color faded from her cheeks. Her lips moved wordlessly as she slipped to the floor, her knees collapsing uselessly beneath her.

"It's okay." Street calmly swept his little sister into his arms and hurried down the hall and out into the fresh air. Rachel trailed helplessly behind.

"Kit? Kitten? It's okay. Come on, now," he coaxed. "Wake up for me." Sinking onto the porch swing, Street settled Kit into his arms, stroking her cheek, brushing her long, raven hair with loving fingers. "Come on back, Kit. I'm here. It's okay, Kitten. You're okay." He rocked her gently and bent to kiss her forehead.

"Street? What should I do?"

"Sit beside me, Rachel," he whispered. "This looks a lot worse than it is."

Rachel perched beside them on the swing, one hand on Street's arm, the other on Kit's tiny hand. "I didn't know . . ."

He shook his head. "It doesn't happen often." Seeing the stricken expression on Rachel's face, Street quickly reassured her. "It's nothing we did, or didn't do, Rachel. These episodes are so unpredictable. Sometimes they happen first thing in the morning, after a good night's sleep. So we can't blame it on her being overtired. They happen when she's hungry, but they also happen after a big meal."

He sighed. "The doctors can't explain it, but it's a lot harder on us than it is on her. She'll come around in a few minutes, and then she'll just want to sleep. And when she wakes, she's good as new."

Kit moaned and stirred restlessly in his arms. "Wake up, Kitten," he coaxed again. "Come on, honey . . . Rachel's here."

Kit's long, dark lashes fluttered briefly before her eyes rolled open. She smiled. "Hi, Rachel."

"Hi, Kit. Are you okay now?"

"Um-humm. But I'm tired . . . soooo tired."

Street hugged his little sister close and smiled at Rachel. "You see? I'll take her back to Riverdale Place. She'll be fine. Don't worry."

Rachel nodded, biting her lip to keep from crying. If only there was something she could do.

Street nudged her arm. "I'm still hungry, you know. Turn off the heat under that spaghetti pot and hold dinner for me, okay? I'll be back as soon as I can."

Dinner? Alone? With Street? "Sounds fine," she whispered, dropping a kiss on Kit's cheek, hoping he didn't notice the tremor in her voice.

"I'll bring us a nice bottle of Chianti," he said, buckling Kit into the Porsche, "and if we're lucky, a loaf of bread, hot from Sandy's oven." He leaned close. "Stop worrying. Kit's fine."

Chapter Fourteen

The sleek black car disappeared down the lane, leaving Rachel standing forlornly in the middle of the yard. How did he do it? she wondered, stumbling up the porch steps to sink weakly onto the swing. He was so calm and collected. Unflappable. While she, on the other hand . . . well, she was definitely flappable. Completely useless. And she'd wondered how a man like him ever came to know the things he did about taking care of people. Well, she didn't have to wonder any more.

She sighed. Maybe it wasn't as easy for him as he tried to make it seem. It was a lot for one person to bear, all alone. Even with the remarkable Sandy to help out.

She hadn't missed the troubled expression that clouded Street's face as he buckled his little sister into the car, the pain in his eyes as he stroked her pale cheek, or how determinedly he'd squared his shoulders afterward. Oh, he'd smiled then, true, and even tried to cheer her up. But that brave front masked a gentler truth. Big, bad Street Wellman was a sensitive, vulnerable man. A man who was willing to trust her, to share the most private parts of his life—

115

"Yikes!" Hurrying to the kitchen, she turned the stove off just as the big pot of water rolled to a boil. Quite a man, that was for sure. With everything else he'd had on his mind, he was the one who'd remembered the pot on the stove. Maybe she'd better make herself presentable before he showed up looking for his dinner.

Freshly showered and perched on the edge of her bed, Rachel brushed her long, strawberry curls until her hair shone in the soft, evening light. She stood and gazed for a moment at the trim figure, the feminine curves, of the woman in the mirror. Dabbing a hint of perfume at her throat, she wondered how it would feel to stand before Street. To feel his eyes, his hands upon her. To touch him—*Stop! It's just dinner, Rachel. That's all. Just dinner.*

So why did her hands tremble when she pulled her favorite dress off its hanger? Why did her heart race when the growl of a finely tuned engine announced his return? "Just dinner," she said aloud, leaning on the windowsill to watch as he wheeled the Porsche into the yard.

He flung the door wide and rose to his feet in one fluid motion, running long fingers through his hair to ease it back into place. He had traded the beach clothes for a pair of khaki pants and a comfortable-looking white cotton shirt that he wore like an old friend, untucked with the sleeves turned up. A nudge from his hip slammed the car door, and Rachel flew downstairs to meet him.

They reached the screen door at the same instant, locked eyes, and stood in mute wonder for just a moment, drinking in the sight of each other.

"Come in," she murmured, struggling to control the tremor in her hands as she pushed wide the door.

Street gazed down into her eyes, aware that the look on his face probably revealed much more than he'd intended. He desperately wanted to touch her face, lose his fingers in that mane of curls, feel her melt into his arms, but he could not. For one thing, his hands were already full of the promised bottle of Chianti and a still-warm loaf of Sandy's round bread. For another, he'd seen the involuntary tremble of Rachel's tiny hands, and even now could sense her nervousness. This was all so new for her. She'd been alone too long. He'd have to take it slow or she'd be off and running all over again.

"You look lovely, Rachel. Sandy sends his love, among other things. Take this, will you?" He turned sideways, extending his elbow, allowing Rachel to relieve him of the brown paper bag gripped snugly underneath. "Sandy wouldn't hear of sending me off for dinner without supplying dessert. I have no idea what's in there, but I can guarantee it'll be delicious."

She smiled, a little more relaxed, he thought, and turned toward the kitchen. Her voice had a quiet, almost breathy quality that left him straining to hear the words she spoke as he followed her down the hall. "The bread smells *sooo* wonderful. I can't wait to try it. Are you hungry?"

"Sure am." *Hungry for you,* he thought, admiring her curves beneath that little breath-of-nothing dress she wore. He wondered if she knew the effect she had on him. *Almost certainly not,* he thought, and sighed as she hid herself behind the kitchen counter.

"How's Kit? Was she feeling any better when you left her?"

"She slept like a baby all the way back to Riverdale Place. I'm not sure she even knew I was there, to tell you the truth. Rina just tucked her into bed and she was out cold." Street leaned heavily against the counter, resting his chin on his hands. "We'll talk about it tomorrow, look at the pictures, and the stones she picked up at the quarry. Then she'll probably remember that she missed her dinner with you."

Rachel brushed his hand with hers. "There'll be another chance, Street. I promised her a spaghetti dinner, and I intend to deliver."

Her smile banished the dark cloud he'd allowed to settle

117

around them and Street responded with a grateful nod. "She's grown very fond of you, Rachel. We all have."

She blushed, turning quickly away to pull Kit's salad from the fridge and light the burner beneath the pasta pot that waited on the stove.

A change of subject seemed prudent. "Where's your corkscrew, Rachel? We'll want this wine to breathe a while."

She crossed the room, her back still toward him, bending low to open a drawer. A soft tumble of curls encircled her face, aglow in the warm light of the kitchen. A well-deserved halo, he mused, undeterred by the decidedly unsaintly thoughts that now bedeviled his mind. *Look away!* Instead, he traced the tempting arch of her neck, the oh-so-lightly tanned arms, the curves beneath the filmy dress that modestly covered all, but hid nothing. *Oh, Rachel.*

She rummaged in one drawer after another, before finally locating the corkscrew and delivering it to Street. Sandy's bread waited on the counter between them. "I can't resist!" she exclaimed, tearing a bite-sized chunk from the loaf and popping it into her mouth. "Mmmmm. Oh, it's *sooo* good!" She tore off another bite and offered it to Street, blushing again as his lips brushed across her fingertips.

Pretending not to notice her embarrassment, Street pulled the cork and set the bottle on the table. "I'll light the candles," he said as she hurried to clear Kit's place setting, then brought a wineglass for each of them.

Street cautiously slipped an arm around her tiny waist. "Can I help?"

"You already have."

He held her a little closer, amazed that she hadn't yet run away. Brushing a hand through her silken hair, he let it linger there for a moment and gently tipped her head upward, forcing her to look at him, bending close to steal a kiss . . . almost.

A sudden clatter from the stove timer sent her flying from his arms. Saved by the bell.

118

Between the uncontrollable trembling of her hands, and the wild pounding of her heart, Rachel feared she'd spill the pot of boiling water and pasta all over the floor. Somehow she managed to dump it into the colander that waited in the sink. *Calm down,* she told herself as she slipped the spaghetti into a bowl and tossed in some of her homemade marinara sauce. She imagined she could feel Street's eyes on her as she worked, and made a concerted effort to ignore the prickling awareness of him that crept up her spine.

"Dinner is served," she said, making her best attempt at a confident smile. Street's persistent gaze followed her across the room.

"Smells wonderful. And I'm starving."

"Mmmm. Me, too." The telephone rang before Rachel had a chance to sit. She knew, from the expression on Street's face, that his first thought was the same as her own. Something had happened to Kit. Crossing the room in two quick strides, she grabbed the receiver. "Hello?"

"Hello, beautiful. Ready for dinner?"

"D-Danny?"

"Well, who else, lovely lady? I can be there in ten minutes. Get your dancing shoes on."

"N-no. I . . . I can't, Danny." She swallowed the sudden lump that rose in her throat at the change in Street's expression. A little flicker of jealousy, perhaps? "Not tonight. I have company."

"Company?" Danny sounded genuinely disappointed. "Anyone I know?"

She didn't answer. He'd never believe it, anyway. "We're just about to sit down for dinner. I'm afraid I'll have to say good-bye."

"You haven't forgotten your promise, have you?"

"No. I haven't forgotten," she replied, wishing she could do just that.

"Call me?"

He sounded a little discouraged, she thought, and she answered as kindly as she could. "I will. 'Bye."

"Sorry about that," she said, watching Street pour wine into their glasses. "When the phone rang, I had a terrible feeling that something might have happened to Kit."

"Same thing occurred to me, I'm afraid. But I'm sure she's fine, Rachel. Probably still sleeping like a baby." Street raised his glass and smiled. "To us," he murmured, touching her goblet with his.

"So . . . who's this Danny of yours? Anyone I should be worried about?"

"Worried?" Feeling suddenly mischievous, Rachel gave in to an impish grin. "I haven't even talked to Danny for ages, Street. Not until last week when you sent him to see me."

"I sent him . . . ?"

"Danny Minelli. Minelli Landscaping?"

"Oh!" This was definitely something to worry about, thought Street, remembering the tall, tanned, and handsome young man who'd been hard at work in his own backyard all week.

"I've known Danny forever, Street," she said, twirling spaghetti around her fork. "We went to kindergarten together, and he's always . . . well, had a crush on me."

A muscle in Street's jaw twitched, and Rachel felt terribly mean for teasing him. "It's not mutual. Never has been. He's a friend. That's all."

"I'd guess, from the way you blushed at whatever young Danny had to say, that he'd like it to be much more than a friendship."

"Won't happen, Street. No way." She laughed. "I promised to have dinner with him. Sort of a bribe, I guess you'd say. It was the only way I could get him to tell me who'd hired him to work on my gardens."

"I see. Well, maybe I'll just have to keep Danny so busy that he won't have the time, or the energy, for wining and dining." He winked, just in case Rachel thought he might be serious. Which, of course, he was.

Rachel laughed and looked away, then focused on his chin and laughed again.

"What?" he demanded.

"Sauce. A big dribble on your chin." She reached across the table, napkin in hand. Street leaned toward her. *"Yikes!"*

Rachel leapt to her feet, knocking her chair to the floor behind her and shrieking again. She'd set the napkin on fire, dragging it past the candles. How incredibly stupid!

Street caught her by the wrist, calmly knocking the napkin out of her hand and trampling it to quell the fire.

"It's all right," he whispered, pulling her into his arms. "No harm done. My face isn't a bit scorched. Honest."

He held her a little closer. "Rachel . . . ?"

She looked up. Street caught her hand and drew her to him. Her eyes fluttered shut against the rush of self-awareness, and Street bent to kiss each fragile lid.

Was he asking too much of her? Too soon? No. This couldn't be wrong. It felt so right. Nuzzling into the softness of her hair, he breathed deeply, memorizing the delicate scent of her, and waiting for some signal of reassurance.

Rachel felt the pounding of his heart, as hard and fast as her own, and dropped her head to rest upon his chest. Her hands explored the hollow of his back, felt a tremor begin and grow. It passed between them, urgent and impatient. She sensed the fire within him, the passion, the promise of things to come, and suddenly understood. Street was fighting to control the longing they shared, afraid of frightening her.

"It's all right," she murmured, gazing up into his gentle, hopeful eyes. She pressed against him until she could move no closer. Tilting her head toward him, she waited for his mouth to cover hers once more.

Street bent to kiss her, tenderly lifting her off her feet as her arms twined tightly around his neck. *Don't stop,* she thought, wishing he could read her mind. *Make it last. A kiss to last forever.* Closing her eyes, she sighed into his mouth as he turned, and turned. Oblivious to where he might be carrying her, Rachel sighed again and snuggled closer, lost in a world where only two hearts beat.

Street sank onto the couch with Rachel still cradled in his arms, their lips still locked in a kiss he was certain only hinted at the depth of passion hiding within the tiny soul he held so close. *I love you,* he thought. And the words, though strange, were no surprise. He did love her. But he couldn't tell her. Not yet. There was business to be done first, to make this right for her.

Slowly opening her eyes, Rachel searched the dimly lit living room in obvious confusion. *What . . . ? How . . . ? I've been swept off my feet,* she thought, delighted by the utterly romantic notion.

Street moved to continue the kiss. His lips found her neck and wandered into the sensitive hollow of her shoulder.

A dizzying wave of feeling burst within her then, like a dam giving way before a flood. It had been so long since anyone had touched her, held her, loved her. When she nestled closer to kiss his throat, to taste the slightly salty skin of his neck and tease his earlobe between her teeth, a groan, low and painful, rumbled from the depths of his being.

"What's wrong?" she asked, almost afraid to hear the answer.

Street folded his arms around her, pulling her close. "I—I'm not prepared for this, Rachel."

The pain in his voice cut like a knife. What was he saying? She stared at him, wide-eyed and fearful.

"It's all right, love," he smiled, winnowing long fingers through her tangled hair.

Love? *He called me love!* Rachel's breath caught in her throat.

"I just . . . didn't . . . expect this. Not that I haven't

dreamt about it, almost every night . . . and hoped . . .''
Street shook his head in obvious dismay.

Suddenly she understood. He'd come for dinner. Just dinner. What was she doing? She'd pushed this on him. Expected too much, too fast. What did he think of her now? And his dinner had gone cold on the table.

Street watched the flash of color cross her cheeks, read the look of horror in her eyes, and knew she had absolutely no idea what he was saying. Or certainly the *wrong* idea. He laughed and Rachel tried to push away, embarrassment giving way to anger.

Street held fast, sheltering her in his arms, showering her face with kisses. ''You're mistaken, my love. I want you. More than you can know.'' He chuckled into her ear. ''I'm sorry,'' he whispered, reading her thoughts at last. ''The timing is wrong. It's a bad idea to move too fast. I only want what's best for you.'' Slipping a hand beneath her chin, he tipped her face upward and dropped a kiss on the tip of her nose. ''What do you suppose good old Sandy sent for our dessert?''

''Chocolate something, I hope.'' She groaned, rolling off the couch. ''Dotty swears it's just as good as kissing.''

Chapter Fifteen

"Rachel, where the heck have you been?" Dotty peered over the rim of her glasses and frowned. "I didn't think you knew how to be late for work."

"I guess I am a wee bit late, aren't I, Dotty? But it's such a wonderful day . . . I just couldn't seem to get myself out of bed. You know how it is." To her surprise, Dotty let that totally un-Rachel-like comment pass without so much as a raised eyebrow.

"All I know is that this place has been absolutely nuts for the last hour, and you missed all the excitement."

"Excitement?" Rachel tried to keep a straight face, but Dotty was obviously itching to tell all. "Okay, I'll bite. What's up?"

"Well, for one thing, Leon's on a rampage, and I'm almost positive it involves Mr. Wellman . . . and you."

It was just dinner. "Really? Why would you think that?"

"Well, maybe because Mr. Wellman called you three times before eight, and again after I got here. I just assumed . . ."

"He . . . called me?"

"I started to say you weren't in yet, but he interrupted. Quite rude, actually. Not at all like himself. Said he had to speak to Leon, right away. And boy, oh, boy, it all hit the fan. Something big is going on, Rachel. Leon's got the boys in there with him now. I have no idea what's up, but I'm going to find out. Just you wait."

Rachel shifted her backpack uneasily from one hand to the other, glancing down the hallway. "Did Leon want to see me, too?"

"No . . ." Dotty sat back in her chair, watching closely as if expecting to discover a clue to the mystery. "But somebody else does."

"What . . . ? Who wants to see me? Dotty, quit playing games."

"All right, already. Gosh, Rachel, I don't need you snapping at me, too. Anyway, this is much more interesting than Leon's bad mood," teased Dotty, fingering a pair of message slips and winking suggestively. "Two messages from Danny Minelli. Says he'll call you at home tonight. Says he can hardly wait."

It seemed to Rachel that it was Dotty herself who could hardly wait.

"Tell me all about him," Dotty demanded. "Are you dating? What's he like? He's got such an intriguing voice."

"Would you like to meet him, Dotty?"

"Would I! Oh, yes, absolutely. I've been *dying* to. My friend at the bank says he's the ultimate hunk. But he always manages to get there before I do in the morning, and then she says, 'Missed him again, ha-ha.' Well, ha-ha on her. I figure he'd have asked her out by now, if he was interested." She giggled, a wicked grin spreading across her face. "I'd just love to make her jealous, Rachel. When do we start?"

Dotty snagged a compact from her desk drawer and, with a quick peek over her shoulder to make sure the coast was clear of partners, studied her image in the mirror. "Do you think I'm . . . his type, Rachel? I mean, do you really think he'd like me?'' She sighed. "I mean, if he's got the hots for you . . .''

"What's that supposed to mean, Dotty?"

"Well, nothing. Just that, well, you're so . . . perfect." Her face fell. "And I'm so . . . not."

"Come off it, Dotty. I'm far from perfect. And don't sell yourself short. You're smart, and pretty, and lots of fun. Sounds exactly like Danny's type to me."

"I dunno, Rachel. I've been in such a rut lately. Do you think I should do something with my hair? It's so . . . yuck!"

Well, the light dawns, thought Rachel, forming her response very carefully. "You might want to try wearing it down. I know Danny likes long hair. And if you're serious about a change, I've always thought something a little more, well, mellow in the color department would be flattering. You have such a beautiful complexion."

"Hmmm. Do you really think so, Rachel?"

She nodded.

"I'll do it!" Dotty pulled the purple band off her bleached blond hair and shook it loose to hang in limp disarray around her shoulders. "Just wait till you see the makeover, Rachel. Danny won't be able to resist." She tucked the compact safely away in her drawer. "So, when do I meet him?"

Oh gosh, now I have to make it happen. "Give me some time to work on it, Dotty. If we're going to do this, we'd better do it right, don't you think?"

The phone rang before Dotty could respond. "Good morning,'' she trilled. "Bristol Foxworth O'Donnell & Kline. How may I help you?" A very brief pause ensued before her sweet reply. "One moment, please."

Dotty leapt to her feet. "It's Mr. Wellman. He wants to talk to you." She offered Rachel the phone with a hopeful arch of her thinly penciled eyebrows. "Find out what's going on."

"I'll take it in my office, Dotty. Thanks."

"Awww, Rachel . . ."

"What?" she asked, backing away as quickly as she could, trying her best to sound bored and businesslike. "I'm sure he just wants to ask me something about his garden. I'm working on the plans for him."

"Really?" Dotty's mood brightened. "Does Leon know?"

"Well, of course he does, Dotty. Why?"

"Oh. Well, I just thought that maybe if you'd been moonlighting or something, and he'd found out . . . well, it might explain things. Don't you think?"

"Have you ever stopped to think that this big mystery you're so worried about just might be a figment of your vivid imagination?" Rachel turned her back and hurried down the hallway, stifling a laugh.

"Rachel? You will tell me what he says, won't you, Rachel? Rachel?"

Quietly but firmly closing the door to her office, Rachel crossed the little room to perch on the edge of her chair. Just the thought of hearing his voice made her knees weak, sent her heart hopscotching. Her hand trembled as she reached to lift the receiver. "Rachel speaking." The words sounded breathless, even to her own ears.

"Are you alone?" She could hear the smile in Street's voice, warm and familiar.

"Not exactly," she whispered as Dotty's shadow flitted past in the hallway. "The walls have ears, you know. How's Kit? Have you spoken to her today?"

"She's just fine, Rachel. I don't think she remembers much about yesterday, but it'll come back to her. Rina said she slept soundly, and ate a huge breakfast. You can stop worrying about our little Kitten now. Okay?"

"I'll try."

Street chuckled. A low, throaty sound that shivered through her body like a cool breeze. "I really enjoyed last night, Rachel. Our little, um, 'discussion' kept me up half

127

the night. We really should talk again. Soon. I hate leaving things unfinished. Don't you?''

Rachel wondered if he could hear her thundering heart through the phone.

''Are you there?'' he whispered.

''I'm . . . remembering . . .'' That was a totally witless thing to say, she thought, but Street seemed to enjoy it, and chuckled again.

''Well, I don't want to keep you from your work, but I need your advice about something.'' His voice grew serious. ''Would you be free for lunch, maybe? Or dinner? There's a problem here, um, in the garden. A big rock . . . or something. Only you have the answer, I'm afraid, Rachel. Will you help?''

A big rock? ''A big rock, eh? That could be a very difficult problem for your garden. I guess I'd better take a look.''

''When?'' he blurted, obviously pleased by her willing participation in his little game.

''I've got a full schedule today, I'm sorry to say. And I'm expected at Riverdale Place for the dinner hour. Would seven be all right?''

''Oh, Rachel, it's a long time to wait. But, then again, seven might be perfect. We'll be able to finish our discussion, pick up where we left off. We could talk the night away.''

''Stop! I've got work to do, and I'm not going to be able to concentrate.''

''Good,'' he growled. ''I'll be thinking about you not concentrating. See you at seven. And Rachel? Don't be late.''

''You're looking especially lovely today, Rach.'' Harry Foxworth punctuated his comment with a waggle of bushy eyebrows and a long, low whistle that, any other day, would have sent Rachel stomping off down the hall, slamming doors behind her. He draped one arm over the water cooler, waiting.

"Thanks, Harry," she chirped, stirring cream and sugar into her coffee, absolutely determined that even he wouldn't spoil her happy mood. "It's an especially lovely day, don't you think?"

Breezing out of the little kitchen and down the hall to her office, Rachel left a very perplexed Harry staring after her, muttering under his breath. "This day," she heard him grumble, "can't possibly get any worse."

Harry was wrong.

Glancing up at the clock as she closed her office door, Rachel sighed. She'd worked right through lunch without a single interruption, but now, at nearly two, her stomach was beginning to grumble. Posted immediately below the clock was her personal To Do list, growing longer by the day. Wellman Enterprises was not the firm's only client, although it had begun to feel that way in the last few weeks.

The thought of Street brought a smile to her lips, but she forced herself to banish his face, and his touch, from her mind. Dreams of last night, and the evening ahead, would put an end to work, and there was simply too much to be done. Taking one last sip of coffee, she set the mug on her desk and leaned over the drafting table again. A final flourish of color completed her master plan drawing for Merrilee Mews, a cooperative housing project in nearby Fairbrook.

"Perfect!" she exclaimed, stepping back to admire the results of her morning's labor. It reminded her why she stayed at BFOK. Personalities and politics aside, the boys were a talented lot. They made a good team.

Settling into her chair, Rachel pulled an apple out of her backpack and crunched off a juicy mouthful. Next on the drawing board was a project she'd been looking forward to for a very long time, the design of a heritage garden for the grounds of Riverdale's museum. It would offer visitors a glimpse into the past, a sort of time capsule of sights, smells, and textures. A very large stack of library books sat on the corner of her desk, and she'd scheduled the rest of the day for research into the lives and gardens of Riverdale's earliest settlers.

"Rachel? Please come to the front." Dotty's voice crackled over the intercom, uncharacteristically abrupt. What now? wondered Rachel, glancing wistfully at the pile of books.

Barry Tarr's voice carried loudly down the hall. "I don't believe this! Who does he think he's dealing with here? I came to see Leon Bristol, not the second string."

"Barry?" Rachel stepped into the hall and waited for him to turn around. He was alone for a change, and seemed smaller without the R.A.T.S. to back him up. "Is there a problem?"

"You're darned right there's a problem!" Barry stalked toward her. "Your boss is refusing to speak to me. Told Dotty to pass me off on you."

"Leon's not seeing anyone today, Barry. He's very busy. But I'd be glad to hear what you have to say. Please, come down to my office."

Without giving him the opportunity to refuse, Rachel took Barry's arm and led him quickly away from Dotty, who looked about ready to strangle someone, given half the chance.

"Would you like some coffee, Barry?"

"No! And you can drop the buddy-buddy act, Rachel. It won't work." He waved a manila envelope under her nose. "I'm dead serious about this."

"I can see you are, Barry." Rachel rounded her desk and sat staring expectantly up at him. "Please, sit down."

"I'll stand." He pulled a sheaf of papers from the envelope. "What do you have to say about this?" he demanded, dropping the documents onto her desk.

Rachel scanned the papers. The name Wellman appeared on nearly every sheet. "Do you want me to read through all this while you stand there, Barry, or will you do us both a favor and tell me what's going on?"

He stared at her for a moment, as if deciding how much she really did or didn't know, then sank onto a chair, wringing his hands. "*Wellmanism,* Rachel. That's what's going on. These are official reports of serious environmental disasters. All courtesy of Wellman's developments. And you want to let him do it here."

She stared at the papers. *Toxic. Destruction. Irreparable.* The words seemed to swim on the pages. "Where did you get these?"

"I have my sources, Rachel. There are people who really do care about the world we live in, you know."

Rachel bit her lip. It was obvious that Barry no longer listed her among those people. "Tell me," she said quietly.

"This—" Barry growled, tapping one page with a crooked index finger. "—this is a nightmare. A Wellman Enterprises development, built right on top of a toxic waste dump. They just filled it in and built new homes. Not 'profitable' to do a proper cleanup, I guess. Now the families living in those houses have sludge leaking into their basements. Nobody knows exactly what it is, or how to clean it up. A nightmare. But I haven't seen it on the news, have you? No. Nobody's heard about it. Why do you suppose that is?" Barry stared at her accusingly.

Rachel felt the blood drain from her face and her skin grow clammy as she slipped another report out of the pile. This couldn't be happening. Not now. "There's more?" she asked, letting the papers fall onto her desk. Her hands seemed about to tremble and she clenched them in her lap, hoping Barry wouldn't notice the effect all this was having on her.

"Oh, yeah. There's more." Barry leaned toward her. "You'll love this one."

His voice droned on, one disaster after another, each sounding worse than the last, until she couldn't bear to hear another word. She had to stop him, say something in Street's defense. *But what? Anything. Just interrupt.* "But—"

131

"No buts, Rachel. These are all well-documented facts. I'm not here for explanations or excuses. I'm here to warn you. And I intend to warn the people of Riverdale." Barry pounded his hands on her desk. "That man's a butcher!"

Forcing herself to stay calm, to speak clearly, she fixed Barry in a steady gaze and said, "I'd like to study these documents. Would you mind if I made copies?" Her voice sounded clear and strong, surprising considering the emotions raging inside.

"Keep them. I've got the originals."

"Fine. You should know, I intend to find out what Mr. Wellman has to say about all this. He plans on making Riverdale his home, you know." She drew a deep breath. "This won't happen here, Barry. He cares about this place. I *know* it."

"You're dreaming, Rachel. Either that, or Wellman's got you, too. Is that it? Are you bought and paid for, too?"

"You know better than that, Barry." *Stay calm!* she warned herself. "I'm trying to keep an open mind, that's all."

"I had no idea you were so naive. Wake up! Before it's too late. Look at this." Rifling through the papers, he pulled out a report, printed on what looked like federal government stationery. "Another Wellman fiasco. Construction runoff from one of their developments silted in a cold-water stream. It destroyed a whole year class of the fishery. The eggs suffocated. If you happen to be a salmon, Rachel, that's *very* serious, because if you're a salmon, you only spawn once. They're gone. Forever." His lips curled back as if he'd tasted something foul. *"Wellmanism!"*

Barry stalked out into the hallway. "Remember, you were warned."

Rachel locked her office door and restlessly paced the floor. What to believe? She'd been unable to defend Street against Barry's attack. A defense would take research, and good answers. Answers she didn't have. And what if Barry was right? The thought turned her stomach.

Sinking into her chair, she began reading, all thoughts of the heritage garden forgotten. She had to understand Barry's accusations. She *had* to.

It took hours to wade through the stack of papers he'd left. None was current, she noticed. Each item dealt with projects completed eight to ten years ago. But she took little comfort in that fact. Street had been in charge of the company for much of that time, too, and many of the problems were just now coming to light. A lot of Barry's material was just malicious anti-Wellman propaganda, but some of it, too much of it, rang frighteningly true.

Dropping her head into her hands, Rachel fought back tears. Tonight was supposed to be perfect, but now? She couldn't keep this from him. And she would not let it hang over their heads. She'd show him everything, hear his side, and they'd put it behind them.

What a surprising thought. She knew that if Barry's timing had been better, if he'd come forward with the information just a day or two earlier, she'd have assumed the worst. But now? She'd just made a giant leap of faith in Street's direction.

It'll be all right, she told herself, aware, for the first time, of just how completely she had begun to trust Street Wellman. Slipping the reports into her backpack, she whispered a prayer that she was right.

Chapter Sixteen

"What's the matter, Rachel?" Kit wrapped both arms around Rachel's neck and gazed into her eyes, obviously concerned. "Don't you like my pictures? Or ... are you sick? Like I was last night?"

"No, sweetie, just tired. And I've got a bit of a headache, too. I had to do a lot of reading this afternoon."

"Bobby can fix headaches, y'know. Bucky, too, but Bobby's better. You should go see him. Tell him I said to fix yours."

"Good idea, Kit. I just might do that," she said, thinking that, in all the world, he was the only one who could fix this particular headache. "Would you like me to brush your hair for you first?"

"Oh, yes, please." Kit flopped onto the little chair in front of the dresser, and tossed her dark hair back over her shoulders. "I like the way you do it, Rachel." She lowered her voice to a whisper. "Better than Rina. She makes ouchies."

As Rachel brushed, careful to avoid any "ouchies," Kit

studied her in the mirror. "How come you look so sad?" she asked at last. "You're not mad at me, are you?"

"Never. Not even for a minute. You know what, though? I think I should go home and have a rest. That's all I need, Kit. Just a little rest."

"Well, okay. But don't forget you promised to take me for a drive to the quarry tomorrow."

"I won't forget, Kit. Don't you worry. We'll just keep going back until we find Old Man Turtle, no matter how many trips we have to make. Okay?"

"Yup! No matter how many." Kit bounced out of her chair. "Y'know what, Rachel? Mrs. Woolsey's reading me a book. I'm gonna go find her. Maybe we can read another chapter." She grinned. "Y'know what else? She makes funny voices when she reads."

"Where are you two headed?" asked Rina as they passed her in the hall. She stopped short at the sight of Rachel's pale face. "What on earth's the matter? Are you sick?"

Kit answered for her. "Rachel's got a headache from too much reading. I told her to go see Bobby. He knows how to fix headaches— Oh, look! There's Mrs. Woolsey. We're reading a book, y'know, Rina."

Rina smiled a little wistfully, as if imagining Bobby's cure for a headache, then abruptly straightened her shoulders and patted Kit's arm. "Off you go, then. Rachel will come see you again when she's feeling better."

With a quick hug for Rachel, Kit was off, skipping happily down the hall toward Mrs. Woolsey.

"Go home, Rachel," ordered Rina. "Take some aspirin, and lie down. You're white as a sheet."

Rachel felt a shiver of déjà vu as she rounded the corner at The Willows. A young couple strolled the lawn, hand in hand, the way she and Peter had so many times. "Can I help you?" she asked, climbing out of the Jeep.

135

"Are you the owner?" The young woman rushed into an explanation the moment Rachel nodded her head. "I hope you don't mind, but we're only here for the day, and I just couldn't leave Riverdale without seeing the old place again."

"You know The Willows?" asked Rachel weakly. Her headache throbbed relentlessly.

"Sure do. It was my granddad's place. I practically lived here every summer when I was growing up." She turned and pointed to the trio of willows by the riverbank. "Granddad planted those, one for each of his kids. And the smaller ones, down the lawn? Those were for me and my brothers." She smiled warmly at Rachel. "I'm so glad you named the place for them. Granddad would be pleased."

Rachel leaned heavily against the Jeep. "It's a beautiful spot, that's for sure. I . . . I know you'd probably love to see the house again, but—"

"Oh, no, we wouldn't dream of imposing, would we, Teddy?" She looked up at the young man again.

"It's just that . . ." Sighing, Rachel raised a hand to shade her eyes from the dazzling sunshine. "I'm really not feeling too well, and—"

"Oh!" Teddy slipped his arm around the young woman. "We're sorry to have bothered you. Amy was just feeling nostalgic." He looked down at her lovingly. "We'll get out of your way."

Poor Amy looked terribly disappointed. "Please. It's quite all right. I don't mind at all if you walk around the grounds. Take your time. And if you're ever in Riverdale again, come back. I'd be happy to give you a tour." She did her best to smile, as a wave of dizziness rolled over her.

"I'd like that," said Amy. "To tell you the truth, we were sort of hoping the place might be for sale."

The unexpected thought of parting with The Willows hit Rachel hard, actually taking her breath away. She stared mutely at the young woman, unable to form any sort of a rational answer.

"I'd love to come home again." Amy sighed and reached into her pocket for a scrap of paper. "This is our phone number," she said hopefully. "Please, if you ever do decide to sell the place, call us first."

Rachel nodded, her fingers trembling as she took the note from Amy's hand. "I'll put this away in a safe place. But really, The Willows means a lot to me. I can't imagine wanting to sell it."

"I understand, but just in case . . ."

Teddy pulled her toward their little car. "Thanks for your hospitality," he said, with a wave of his hand. "We'll be going. Hope you feel better soon."

Me, too, thought Rachel, as she struggled up the porch steps and into the house. It was cool, soothingly dark inside, and she wandered through to the kitchen, dropping her backpack on the hall floor. She poured a cold glass of water and took two aspirins from the cupboard, gulping them as she sank onto a chair, and then holding the cool glass against her forehead.

She stared at the slip of paper in her hand. *Ted and Amy Watson.* A tear trickled down her cheek. Would it ever stop hurting? she wondered. Would she ever be able to think of Peter without crying? Pushing the water glass away, she dropped her head onto her arms and let the tears fall.

Sandy tweaked the candle wicks to attention, fluffed the napkins into little puffs in the wineglasses, and stood back, hands on hips, to admire his table.

"It's perfect, Sandy," said Street from the doorway. "The table, the food, the flowers, the house . . . everything. You're stalling, old man. Get out of here, will you . . . *please?*"

Sandy chuckled. "My boy, I'm going to let that pass because I know you're nervous."

"Nervous? I am not—"

"Oh, yes you are. Worse than your first date, back in high school. What was her name . . . ?"

"Sandy!"

"I'm going, I'm going. Now don't forget to drizzle a little lemon on the salmon, and—"

"I know. You've told me twenty times. It'll be perfect."

Sandy patted Street's arm as they walked to the front door. "I couldn't be more pleased that you and Rachel have finally found each other, my boy. Have a wonderful time. I'll see you tomorrow." Grabbing an overnight bag from a chair by the door, Sandy hurried to his car.

"Thanks," Street called after him. "For everything, I mean. It's—"

"Not another word, my boy. Glad to do it. Frankly, I'm looking forward to a night on my own."

Sandy waved cheerfully as he backed out onto the road and sped away, leaving Street standing on the front step, staring at his watch.

Five after seven. She'll be arriving any minute, he thought, gazing hopefully down the road in the direction of The Willows. Not a car in sight. He paced down the hall to the kitchen, pulled the cork from a bottle of Châteauneuf, and lit the candles.

Seven-fifteen. She was teasing. Street stalked back to the living room window to stare into the distance, remembering the last words he'd spoken to her that morning. "Don't be late."

By seven-thirty he was pacing the room, suddenly certain that something was wrong. Racing through to the kitchen, he grabbed the phone off the hook and dialed Riverdale Place. Rina's efficient voice answered.

"Rina, it's Bobby. How's my sister tonight?"

"Just fine. I saw her a bit earlier in the social room, reading a book with one of the older residents. Apparently dinner was one of her favorites. She had seconds. Shall I call her to the phone?"

"No, no. Don't bother her. I was just concerned, that's

138

all. Um . . . was Rachel in to see her today? I'd like to speak with her, if she happens to be there.''

"Rachel was in earlier. She and Kit get along so well, don't they?'' When he didn't respond, Rina continued. "Anyway, poor Rachel was feeling ill, and I sent her home early. She looked quite ghastly. If you really need to talk to her, I'd suggest you wait till tomorrow.''

Street dropped the phone into the cradle and raced through the house. The sudden feeling of dread that gripped him at the thought that Rachel might be in trouble drove him as close to absolute panic as he ever wanted to come. Until now, only Kit had been able to elicit that sort of reaction from him. A sickening, heart-stopping fear. Until now.

Wheeling to a halt on the front lawn of The Willows, it occurred to Street that he couldn't remember anything of the trip out from town, or of navigating the winding lane. He was being irrational. Rachel was probably fine, just running a little late. But, irrational or not, every instinct had told him to find her. Fast. And he had. It was 7:43.

She'd left the door unlocked. Anybody could have walked in on her . . . taken her . . . hurt her. "Rachel?'' The rising panic he felt colored his voice as he called her name. There was no response.

Street tore through the hallway to the kitchen, mindlessly kicking her backpack out of the way as he passed. A glass of water, half empty, stood in a puddle in the center of the table. "Rachel?'' The house was eerily quiet.

Back down the hall he ran, rounding the corner to take the stairs two at a time. His heart pounded as he flew the last few paces to the end of the hall, to the door of her room.

"Rachel?'' He stared at her for a moment, lying so silent and still on the bed, then forced himself into motion again. Crossing the room in two long strides, he dropped to his knees at her side. His hand trembled as he reached to touch her. "Please let her be all right." Her tiny waist rose and fell, almost imperceptibly, beneath his hand. She was breathing, slow and steady, just asleep. Street heaved a sigh of relief as he spoke her name again.

"Rachel? It's me." He brushed away the damp cloth she'd draped across her eyes, dropped a gentle kiss on her lips. "Are you all right? I was so worried . . ."

Her eyes fluttered as she rolled into his arms.

"Mmmmm." Still half-asleep, she nestled her head against his chest. It would be wonderful to wake up this way all the time, she thought, shivering with pleasure as his fingers smoothed the hair away from her face. "I'm sorry I frightened you," she whispered. "It was a rough day and . . . I had a terrible headache. I just wanted to rest for a few minutes . . . there was plenty of time, I thought. Guess I fell asleep."

Street's lips brushed gently across her forehead. "Don't be sorry. Are you feeling better now? Can I get you anything?"

Rachel eased up onto one elbow and opened her eyes. "No. I'm feeling much better. The headache's gone." She swung her legs over the edge of the bed and stretched, dropping both arms around Street's neck.

"Really. I'm fine. And if it's not too late . . . We did have plans for the evening, didn't we?"

"Indeed we did," he said with a chuckle. "Shall we?"

Rising to his feet, Street drew her close, gazing down into her eyes with a look that told her, more than any words could have, how very much she meant to him.

Rachel stood on tiptoe, her face tilted upward, lips parted in anticipation of the kiss he seemed poised to deliver, when the phone jangled abruptly. She froze. *Not Danny again. Not now.*

Pulling away, she dove for the receiver, gasping a breathless "Hello?" before it could ring the second time.

"Rachel? It's Rina."

"Rina?" Rachel's heart slammed into her throat. *Kit!*

Something was wrong. Rina's voice was carefully metered, but an undercurrent of alarm was clearly evident in those few words she'd spoken.

"What is it, Rina? What's wrong?"

Street's face had blanched at the mention of Rina's name, and Rachel reached for his hand, holding tight. His skin felt clammy and, as she watched, the muscle in his jaw began to twitch.

"It's Kit. She's gone." Rina's voice trembled. "Rachel, we've combed the grounds, and the building. She's just disappeared. I can't reach Mr. Buchanan; there's no answer at his house. The police are on the way . . . Rachel, I just thought, being so close to Kit, you might have some idea where to look."

"I'm on my way. We'll find her. Rina, we *have* to find her."

Rachel blurted out the story as she and Street ran down the stairs and out the front door. "They've lost her, Street. Where's Sandy? Rina said she can't reach him." Her voice cracked and tears began to trickle down her cheeks. "Oh, dear Lord, please, *please* let her be all right."

Street wrenched open the car door and threw himself behind the wheel. Rachel saw his hand shake as he turned the key in the ignition. He hadn't uttered a word, or even looked at her. It was as if action was all that held him together. His jaw twitched again as he rammed the Porsche into gear.

Rachel gripped the armrests until her knuckles whitened. She squeezed her eyes shut. Her stomach lurched as the car hurtled around the hairpin curves of the lane, and barreled onto the highway at breakneck speed.

Feeling every second as an hour, she focused on the road ahead, mentally willing the car to fly. All the horrible possibilities flooded her mind. Where would Kit go? To the ravine again? To the river? *Please, no!*

Street sat, hunched over the wheel, beads of perspiration breaking on his brow and upper lip. She could feel his fear, and rested a trembling hand on his arm as they sped down the driveway at Riverdale Place. The car squealed to a stop beside a police cruiser.

Taking the stairs three to a stride, Street was through the doors and down the hall, with Rachel close behind.

"Mr. Wel—uh, Bobby, thank goodness you're here." Rina rushed toward them. "And Rachel. Thank you so much for coming."

Tight-lipped and ashen, Street spoke for the first time. "Drop the 'Bobby,' Rina. We're beyond all that now. Rachel knows who I am, and we've got to tell the police *everything*. Kit's life could be at stake. Where are they?"

"They're out searching the grounds, Mr. Wellman. They've searched her room already, and we've got staff going over every inch of the place for the third time." She leaned briefly against the wall, her face drawn with worry, and then hurried toward the front door. "The volunteer fire department's been called and they're on their way to help with the search. I have to meet them."

Street looked at Rachel, the dreadful reality of the situation sinking in. This was a small town. No teams of men at the ready. No specialized search-and-rescue unit. Just a couple of cops and the volunteers. "We have to find her, Rachel." His voice cracked and he slumped against the desk. "They threatened to take her . . . before. I can't believe this is happening."

"Mr. Wellman?"

All eyes turned to the front door, as Police Chief Ritchie's voice boomed again. "Where's Mr. Wellman?" The chief strode to the central desk, red-faced and slightly out of breath as Street turned to identify himself.

"Chief Ritchie," said the big man, dropping his notebook on the desk. "We're searching the grounds. We need any information you can give us. *Anything*. I understand the girl's wandered off before?"

"It may be a little more complicated than that, I'm afraid." Street's voice was tightly controlled. "There've

142

been threats of kidnapping in the past, though not recently, and certainly not since we've been in Riverdale. We've tried to shield her by using our mother's name for the admission records. No one, except the attending doctor and Rina, knows that she's my sister. But that's not important anymore. Have you found anything? Anything at all?''

Chief Ritchie shook his head. ''Nothing. Certainly nothing to suggest foul play. We hoped you might be able to shed some light on your sister's habits. Sometimes a tiny detail will turn an investigation around. When did you see her last?''

''This morning. I stopped by after breakfast. She . . . she wasn't well last night, and I—I was worried.'' He sighed. ''She seemed fine, though, and perfectly happy.''

''I saw her at five-thirty.'' Rachel hugged herself tightly to stop the trembling that seemed to have overtaken her whole body. ''She was excited about a book she's been reading with Mrs. Woolsey. She seemed fine—a little vague about yesterday, but . . . Oh, if only I'd stayed a little longer. She might still be here!''

''We can't blame ourselves,'' said Street, as much to reassure himself as for her sake. ''It's not your fault.''

''He's right, Rachel.'' Chief Ritchie left no room for discussion. ''The important thing now is to find her. The whys and wherefores can wait till later.''

''She loves to walk around the grounds, Chief,'' said Rachel, remembering the shine in Kit's eyes the first time she'd seen the swing in the big old maple. ''When she wandered off before, I found her at the top of the ravine, sound asleep on the grass. She . . . she doesn't realize how dangerous it can be out there. There's no way she could know how big the woods are out back, or how easy it is to get lost. She just wouldn't think of it. What if she fell down that big hill?''

Chief Ritchie tramped toward the door. ''We'll search the woods, Rachel, while the light holds.'' He checked his watch and muttered, ''Not much time . . .''

Street seemed lost. "I—I have to find Sandy," he said, and reached across Rina's desk for the phone. His hand shook as he punched in the number.

"I want to check her room, Street. Maybe I'll see something the police didn't notice."

Nodding, Street leaned wearily on the desk. "*Answer*," he hissed into the phone. "Sandy, where are you?"

"Aahhhhh. This is the life." Sandy sighed contentedly, surveying the mounds of bubbles that churned around him in the deliciously warm, rose-scented water of Fairbrook Spa's finest suite.

He took a long, luxurious, thirst-quenching sip of the fruit nectar room service had delivered, and leaned back, adjusting his headphones. Closing his eyes, he raised both hands, tapping an imaginary baton on an imaginary podium as he prepared to lead the London Philharmonic Orchestra in a spirited rendition of—"*Drat!*"

Nestled in a soft white bathrobe on the chair next to the tub, his cellular phone shrilled demandingly.

"Drat," he said again. "I was just beginning to unwind." Sandy snagged the phone with one hand, momentarily lowering his baton, and snapped an impatient response. "Yes? What is it?"

"It's me." The tension in Street's voice sent a shiver down Sandy's back.

"Street? What's wrong?"

"I . . . I'm at Riverdale Place. Sandy, we need you. Kit's missing."

Chapter Seventeen

"**H**ave the police been called?" Sandy was composed and thinking clearly, as was his way in every emergency. Even as he spoke, he was climbing from the tub, the phone still pressed against his ear.

"Yes, they're here. The volunteer firefighters, too. They've been searching the grounds, and Rachel's checking Kit's room right now. Maybe she'll see something the police missed." His voice cracked. Had the unthinkable happened? "Sandy, what if it's . . ."

"Nonsense, dear boy. There hasn't been the slightest hint of anything shady to do with our girl since we've been here. No. It's far more likely that she's wandered off again. Never mind all this chatter, Bobby. *Get moving.* I'm practically on my way. Ten minutes, tops, and I'll be out of here."

Sandy hardly bothered to towel away the lingering bubbles before pulling on his clothes. He rushed to the front desk, leaving his suite in a shambles.

"Emergency, I'm afraid," he called to the clerk at the desk. "I'll be back to pick up my things. No time to explain.'' He was out into the parking lot and in his car before the astonished woman could even form an answer.

Ordinarily, the drive from Fairbrook would take an hour. Not today, though. The car would fly. The silver sedan hugged the road like a ghostly apparition. Curves and bends and miles of road disappeared under the wheels, and time seemed suspended. Only then, with nothing to do but think and drive, did Sandy allow himself to ponder the possibilities.

How could Kit have wandered off again, with all those nurses keeping an eye on her? After all the talks he'd had with her about telling someone before she did anything, or went anywhere? ''Not that Kit remembers what you've said for more than five seconds after you've said it,'' he said with a sigh.

No, he thought, she couldn't be held accountable for her actions. He smiled sadly to himself as he forced the car around another right-angle curve at colossal speed. The only things Kit seemed able to remember were to do with turtles, and fishing, and spending time with Bobby. And, more recently, with Rachel.

Of course! The quarry! That was where she'd be. And all he had to do was call Street and tell him. He fumbled for his phone. Not there. He had rushed out so quickly, he'd left it at the spa. No time to turn back now. Pushing his foot down hard on the accelerator, he sped down the road toward Riverdale Place.

At the same time Street was hanging up the phone, Rachel was running toward him from Kit's room, a little bundle of photos in her hand. They were the Polaroid shots of the day before, taken as the three of them had laughed and splashed and looked for Old Man Turtle at the quarry.

''Look what I found. Kit showed them to me . . . when I was here this afternoon.'' Not only her voice, but her whole body shook, and she leaned against him for support. ''Street . . . that *has* to be where she's gone.''

146

Street reached for the photos. ''We'd better tell the chief. Come on, Rachel.''

Hand in hand, they tore through the front door and around the corner of the building. No search party in sight, but there wasn't a second to lose. It was nearly dark.

''Come on, Street, we can be there in five minutes.'' She ran to the Porsche and threw herself inside.

''You read my mind,'' he answered, jumping into the driver's seat and firing up the engine.

There was great relief in positive action, and neither spoke as they rocketed along the highway. The quarry. That had to be where Kit had gone. There were simply no other options. At least, none that the two of them were willing to consider.

In the failing light, Street's face looked drawn, etched with worry. Rachel felt a wave of love and compassion. If only she could take away his pain. . . .

''It'll be all right,'' she murmured, resting her hand on his arm. ''We'll find her. I *know* we will.''

Street's expression softened a little as he covered her hand with his. ''Rachel, I—I don't know how I could go through this without you. But I—I'm sorry . . . all I can think about is Kit.'' He put his hand back on the wheel and pushed the car harder, driving in tense silence until the chain across Quarry Road stopped them.

''The key's in the glove box,'' said Street. ''Get the chain, will you? And just leave it open; we might need to get out in a hurry.''

Rachel was back in the car before the chain hit the ground, and they careened down the road, parking as close as they could to Quarry Lake.

A brief search of the trunk turned up a flashlight that still had a little power left in its battery. Street shone the feeble beam in front of them, not much to light the way, but better than nothing.

''She probably would have retraced her steps, don't you think? Gone to the spot where we had our picnic?'' Rachel

147

stumbled, caught his arm, and held tight. There were so many hazards in this place, even in daylight. If Kit was here, all alone in the dark, she'd be terrified. What if she ran? Tripped and fell?

"Street, what was that? No, over there." Closing her hand around his, she aimed the flashlight into the gloom. "Do you see something . . . there . . ."

Dropping to her knees, Rachel picked up the remnants of a wildflower bouquet. "She was here, Street, right at this very spot." Her voice trembled. Neither one of them spoke the fear that was foremost in their minds. *Where was she now?*

Street knelt to touch the flowers. "Buttercups and daisies. Kit's favorites. Oh, no . . ."

"Street. *Street!* She must have gone to the lake."

He was on his way, running, before the words were out of her mouth. The light from his flashlight was almost nonexistent now, and Rachel stumbled again before she caught up, catching his hand in hers. They were reduced to practically feeling their way toward the water.

"Kit?" Street's voice rang out through the darkness, strong and firm. "Kitten? Are you here?" He might have been playing a game of hide-and-seek, judging by his tone.

Rachel followed his lead. "Kit? Where are you, sweetie? We want to take you home now." There was no reply.

Street squeezed her arm gently. "Don't give up, Rachel. I *know* she's here." He called again, louder this time. "Kitten! It's time to go home now."

A faint sound, like something moving, barely audible above the gentle lapping of water against the shore. Then, a tiny voice. "Bobby?"

"Kit? I'm here. Don't move, just stay where you are. Rachel and I will come to you. Keep calling!"

"Bobby, where are you? I'm scared," sobbed Kit. "Bobby . . . come get me . . . I wanna go home!"

The flashlight chose that moment to give up the ghost.

148

The only light was a faint twinkle of distant stars. No help at all.

"We're coming, Kitten," called Street, clutching Rachel's hand and moving purposefully along the shore. "Just keep talking, okay, Kit? Talk to me."

"Don't cry, Kit," said Rachel. "We're here now. I guess we'll have to come back in the daytime, what do you say? The way we talked about? You know—together?"

"I w-wanted to, Rachel. *Honest.* I j-just . . . I just came today instead." She drew a long, ragged breath and shuddered through another sob. "I—I'm s-sorry."

Rachel felt the tears burn in her own eyes. "Oh, sweetie, you don't have to be sorry—" In that instant, they all but tripped over Kit. In what seemed like a single movement, they dropped to the ground beside her, folding her safe in their arms, hugging her tight.

Kit held on as if she'd never let go.

"Oh, Bobby," she cried, "I was a-afraid you lost me. I . . . I . . . I wanna go home. P-please, Bobby. P-please, take me home."

"Shhhh. It's okay, Kitten." Street's voice, husky with emotion, was muffled by the mass of Kit's hair on his face. "Everything's fine. You're all right, and we'll soon have you tucked up in bed. Just relax."

"Rachel, you won't leave me, will you?"

"Of course not, Kit. I'll always be here if you need me." She bit her lip, trying to stem the sob that rose from her chest. It was true. She *would* always be there for Kit, no matter what. Pulling off her sweater, she wrapped it tenderly around Kit's shoulders. "Come on," she said, gently touching Street's arm. "Let's get her back where she belongs."

"Where am I?" Kit began to tremble as the Porsche drew to a halt in the parking lot at Riverdale Place. She grabbed hold of Rachel's arm and clung tight, as if it were a lifeboat and she were drowning.

149

There were flashing lights, and people running, and far too much excitement for poor Kit to handle. Even the familiar sight of Rina's face didn't calm her down, and she refused to relinquish her death-grip hold on Rachel's arm. Turning away from the crush of people milling around the car, she hid her face in obvious terror. "Please," she begged, "make them go away." Her voice began to shake. "M-make them go . . . p-please."

Rina took immediate charge, addressing Street directly. "I think we'd better get this young lady to her room. If you'd see to that, Mr. Wellman, I'll look after the rest of this rabble. There's no need for any more disruption here tonight." She turned to face the crowd of onlookers and official searchers, and waved her hands at them as though they were a flock of unruly chickens. "Move along," she said half sternly, half smiling. "It's time everyone went home, or back to bed. Let's give Mr. Wellman some space."

There were more than a few murmurs of surprise at the mention of Street's name, but the crowd parted easily to let him pass, carrying his sister, with Rachel close at his side.

Kit's cranky grumblings were almost audible, as were Street's soothing words to the tiny figure he held so lovingly in his arms. A ripple of whispers ran through the crowd as they passed, the sound of Riverdale's rumor mill kicking into high gear. Not that Street and Rachel could have cared. Their only concern at the moment was how to get Kit settled down for the night. A task which was proving a trifle difficult. She refused to be left alone.

"No! I won't stay here! I won't! I hate it here!" Her big brother, as usual, was unflappable.

"Now Kitten, you know you love it here. You've had quite an adventure, and you need to get some rest. Rachel and I are going to tuck you in and stay right here with you until you're fast asleep. Everything will be fine."

Kit was unconvinced. "I w-want Rachel to stay. All night. I can't sleep if she doesn't."

"All right, sweetie, all right. We'll just get Rina to find a cot for me and I'll stay right here beside you. Would that help you sleep?"

Kit turned a tear-streaked face to Rachel, and attempted a smile. "Uh-huh, I . . . I think so."

"Then it's settled," she said, before Street could protest. "Let's get you washed up a bit while Bobby goes to find me a bed, okay?"

"O-okay," said Kit, stifling a huge yawn.

Rachel rested her hand on Street's arm, gently propelling him out the door. "Why don't you go see what you can rustle up for me? There's no point arguing. Kit needs me and I'm staying."

Street touched her cheek. "Rachel, we need to talk. There . . . there are a few things—"

"First things first," she said, feeling her heart sink into her shoes at the thought of all that would have to be asked, and answered. "We can talk after Kit goes to sleep."

He seemed about to say something else, then to think better of it, and turned away, dragging his feet as if too exhausted to say another word. Rachel called after him. "Street, I didn't mean—" But he didn't hear, or didn't answer.

Had they reached an impasse? she wondered. Both needing to talk, both afraid, both putting Kit first . . . at least for tonight?

She watched him stop at the nurses station, watched his shoulders sag when Chief Ritchie approached with a crowd of curious staff and residents. He looked so tired, so defeated.

Sandy Buchanan burst through the front door then, and tore down the hall, wild-eyed at first, then weak with relief. "Thank goodness," she heard him say, as he threw his arms around Street.

"Yes, thank goodness," she repeated, brushing a tear

from her eye and attempting an almost-bright face for Kit. "Come on, sweetie, let's get you changed and washed, okay?"

Kit was cranky and tired, her black hair in bird's-nest disarray around her face. "What's wrong with you, Rachel? You look awful," she snapped, frowning as she reached under her pillow for her pajamas. "You promised you'd stay. And . . . and I don't want the lights out, okay? It was too dark at that place. I don't like it dark. And I don't wanna get washed, either. I'll just wait till tomorrow." Her pout was very much in evidence, and Rachel sighed.

"No way, kiddo. Leaving the lights on is fine with me, but you don't get out of a wash and brush-up that easily. And anyway, you got a few bumps and scrapes on your adventure. We'd better fix them up, don't you think?"

With Kit washed, and bandaged, and snug in her bed, Rachel slumped wearily into a chair, resting her head on her hand. *Too much,* she thought. Too much of everything today. And there was still more to figure out before it was finally over. That talk with Street, for one thing—

A shadow loomed in the doorway. It was Street, arms full of blankets and a pillow, with a camp cot tucked under his elbow. He smiled wryly. "This is all I could find. I hope you'll be able to sleep on it." Unfolding the cot, he frowned doubtfully. "Guess it'll have to do," he muttered.

"Bobby, it's too noisy in here. I can't sleep." Kit tossed in her bed, lifting her head off the pillow to stare balefully at her brother. "Too noisy," she repeated, just in case he'd missed the point.

"Sorry, Kitten, I didn't mean to disturb you. Why don't we just turn off—"

"No!" cried Rachel and Kit in unison.

Street jerked his hand away from the lamp. "Sorry again." He groaned, looking more downcast than Rachel had ever seen him.

Standing, she reached for his hand. "No, Street, *we're*

sorry. For yelling. It's just that, well, Kit's had enough darkness for tonight. It's okay . . . really.''

Street pulled her body tightly against his own. "Oh, Rachel, I want so much for everything to be okay. Especially everything between you and me. You have no idea how much I want that.''

"*Shhhhhhh!*" hissed Kit, from beneath her blanket.

Rachel lowered her voice to a pitch above a whisper. "Doesn't look like we're going to get much of a chance to talk. I promised Kit I wouldn't leave. Unless . . . where's Sandy? Could he . . . ?''

"Sorry, love. Poor Sandy was a wreck. I sent him home.''

She sighed. "There's so much I need to ask you.''

Street looked down into the face of the woman he loved, into dark-rimmed eyes, clouded with exhaustion. Her pale skin had taken on an almost ghostly whiteness. And it was all his fault. If only he had time to explain, to erase the worry. Even just a little more time.

Instead, he held her close again, pressing his face against her hair, whispering her name. "Rachel, I . . . I have to leave now.'' The shock and disbelief that flashed across her face cut deeper than any knife.

"Leave? What . . . ? Street, I—I don't understand. What's going on?'' Her whispered words were spoken in shaky sentences. "Wh-where are you going?''

"I'm so sorry, Rachel. Sorrier than you'll ever know. But I have to catch a flight to Baltimore in two hours. I thought . . . I thought we'd have more time together. I really wanted us to talk . . . about what's happening here in Riverdale . . . what's happening with us, but . . . we've just run out of time. I'm sorry.'' He groped for words to comfort her. There were none.

"Sorry?'' she repeated. "You're sorry?'' She pulled away, and sat heavily on the chair by Kit's bed. "I—I don't understand. I'm so tired and confused . . . I can't even think. And you're leaving town? For how long, Street?''

The question was a challenge of sorts, and he winced at the hurt look in her eyes. No warmth and compassion there for him now. Only suspicion, pain . . . fear. He felt powerless to explain.

"At least a week, I'm afraid. Four more stops after Baltimore. But I'll be back just as soon as I can. And then . . . then I won't go away again. I promise you that, Rachel." He stared down at the tile floor, glanced at his watch, and gave an exasperated sigh. It was past midnight. "It wasn't supposed to be this way. Look, I'm late. I've got to go. Rachel, you *have* to trust me."

"Do I? Are you always going to run away, just when things get difficult?" She kept her voice low, but her anger was unmistakable.

"Come on, Rachel, that's not fair." *Don't make me leave you like this!* "Look, I'll phone you tomorrow at work. We'll talk then, okay?"

"Sure, whatever." She looked up. Cool, glassy-eyed. "You'd better get going, I guess, or you'll miss your flight."

Chapter Eighteen

"Make a fist, dear girl, and for goodness' sake, put some *oomph* into it!" Sandy Buchanan gave Rachel a little nudge for encouragement. "Like this," he said, giving a determined grunt as he drove his fist into a lump of bread dough. "I'm telling you, my dear, it's very therapeutic. Particularly if you try imagining a face on it. For instance, this loaf has beady little R.A.T.S. eyes."

Rachel giggled in spite of herself, balled up her fist, and gave her lump of dough a mighty punch. In her mind's eye, a suggestion of Harry Foxworth's leer appeared. She pounded again, harder this time. When Barry Tarr stared up at her, mouthing the words "you've been warned," she gave in to her anger and fear, furiously pummeling the dough with both hands, out of control.

Sandy finally stopped her, catching her fists in his hands. "Rachel," he said, looking askance at the flat and lifeless mass, "I think you've killed it." She promptly burst into tears.

"Oh, dear. Oh, Rachel . . . it's only an old lump of bread

155

dough, dear." Sandy wrung his hands. "Oh, please. I didn't mean . . ."

"I—I'm so s-sorry, Sandy." She sobbed. "I . . . d-don't . . . I . . . can't . . ." Sinking onto a chair, she made a futile swipe at the tears, leaving her face streaked with flour.

Sandy pulled a chair close, resting his hand on her knee. "It's all right, dear. You just have a good cry. Let it out." He sighed, terribly discomfited by the sweet, lovely woman who sat sobbing at his kitchen table. At the same time, though, he was happily aware that he was the one she'd sought out. He was the one she'd chosen to share this difficult morning.

He stared spitefully at the newspaper she'd left on the table. A dreadful old photo of Street, his face twisted into an angry snarl, stared back at him from the front page of the Riverdale *Clarion.* Darned reporters! The vitriolic attack on Wellman Enterprises, and Street in particular, was peppered with quotes from Barry Tarr, and other "reliable sources." Sandy turned the paper facedown. "Reliable sources" indeed. Why had nobody bothered to seek out the truth?

And, if that wasn't bad enough, they'd stopped the presses for a late addition, a sidebar about Kit's brief disappearance last night. They'd made it seem somehow scandalous that the poor child was at Riverdale Place under "an assumed name." Sandy clenched his teeth. He would not let them hurt her. Never again!

All this was going to be especially hard on Street. He'd managed to convince himself that Riverdale was different. Good people, he'd said. Sandy was unconvinced. Except for Rachel, of course. She was the very best sort of person.

He pulled a handkerchief from his pocket and tucked it into her hand. "I think we need a cup of tea, don't you, my dear?"

"Y-yes. Tea would be good, I think."

"I'll put the kettle on, and then we'll have a good, long

talk about all of this. There are things you need to know, Rachel.''

Taking a deep breath that ended in a long, shuddering sigh, Rachel blotted her face with Sandy's handkerchief and tried to sit up straight. Street no longer stared up at her from the newspaper; Sandy had wisely folded it away. But the table . . . she hadn't really noticed it before, so elegantly laid out. Dinner for two. The dinner that never happened.

Biting her lip against the renewed threat of tears, she gazed at the single white rose that lay, poignantly wilted, on one of the dinner plates. Intended for her? She picked it up with trembling fingers and carried it to the sink.

Sandy was humming a tuneless little song, and trying his best to salvage the batch of bread he'd been kneading when she'd made her unexpected arrival. ''Oh, dear,'' he murmured, glancing at the flower. ''Tepid water, Rachel. Just put the poor thing right in the sink, with tepid water. Then leave it to me.'' He winked. ''I know an old florist's secret that just might save the day. You'll have that little rose to take home. I can almost guarantee it.''

''Are there any mysteries of life that you don't have a secret solution for?'' Rachel ran water into the sink and made her best attempt at a smile in his direction.

He grinned. ''None that I can think of offhand, my dear.''

''Didn't think so.'' The smile came a bit easier that time, and she leaned on the counter, watching him scrape what was left of her murdered dough into the compost bin. ''Sorry about that. I imagined I could see Barry's face, and I guess I just . . . lost it.''

''Therapy, my dear. Every bit as worthwhile a use for my bread as sandwiches or toast.'' Sandy chuckled. ''Truth be told, I've done the same thing myself, on more than one occasion.''

''He warned me, you know.'' Rachel spoke softly, unable to look Sandy in the face.

''Who warned you? About what?''

157

"Barry Tarr. He . . . he came to the office yesterday. He wanted to see Leon, but . . . well, anyway, he wound up in my office with—" Rachel hurried across the room to pull the envelope from her backpack. "With this." She placed it hesitantly on the counter, and waited while Sandy removed the contents and scanned each page.

"Well. I see." He dropped the pages onto the counter and stared at them, then at Rachel, as if deciding what to do.

"I told him he was wrong about Street. Honestly, Sandy, you've got to believe me. I wanted to talk to Street about it. I was going to show him these last night, and we'd talk about it . . . decide what to do. I know there's another side to all this, Sandy, and I believe in Street. I really do. But I . . . we . . . we never got the chance to talk about it, because Kit was missing, and then Street was so upset, and then he said he had to go away, and I . . . I . . ."

Close to tears again, she impatiently rubbed her eyes. "I didn't know that Barry had already gone to the *Clarion*. Really, I didn't." Her voice shook. "I didn't know, and now I can't talk to Street about it, and . . . and what if he thinks I . . . oh, Sandy, the article mentions sources at BFOK. What if he thinks I had something to do with it?"

"Oh, my dear Rachel, no. Don't think that. Not for a minute. Street knew the *Clarion* was on to something. One of their reporters woke Leon Bristol up in the wee hours of Monday morning, fishing for comments on the story. It was already written, mind you. Anyway, Street laid down the law yesterday. Told Leon he was to say nothing, and do nothing. I gather your boss was none too impressed." Sandy sighed. "Street's tactics can be hard to accept, I know that from personal experience. But the point is, Rachel, he knew what was coming. He'd planned to explain it all to you last night, before—" He shook his head woefully. "It's the trashy little story about Kit that he's going to take badly, I'm afraid. He had such hopes for her, for this place."

158

"Sandy, you don't think he'll . . ." She swallowed hard, still battling tears. "He will come back, won't he?"

"Of course. You really are in love with him, aren't you, *cara mia?*" Sandy took her hand, patting it gently. "Love does have a way of opening the eyes. Go and sit. I'll fix our tea, and then there's something I want to show you."

Rachel sank onto a chair at the kitchen table, a tide of relief washing over her. Street had intended to explain things, but never got the chance. And she'd been so mean to him last night. She should have held him, told him she really did believe in him. But at least Sandy knew the truth.

The little man bustled across the room to set the tea tray on the table and then disappeared into the hallway. She could hear him muttering to himself as he rummaged around in a closet.

"Aha! I knew it had to be here." The well-used file box that Sandy dragged into the kitchen was bulging at the seams with an assortment of magazines, file folders, and, lying on top of everything, one very large scrapbook. "This is it, my dear. Pour the tea, won't you, just a wee touch of milk for me, while I try to find . . ." He flipped through the pages. "There!"

Sandy passed the scrapbook across the table, pointing to a clipping, carefully pasted to the page. A young boy, freckle-faced and grinning, stood knee-deep in a stream, fly-fishing. IMPOSSIBLE DREAM announced the headline. NEW DEVELOPMENT BRINGS FISHERY TO DRAINAGE DITCH.

Sipping her tea, Rachel read the short article, full of kind words about a new subdivision, a trout stream, and the man behind it all, Street Wellman.

"There's more," said Sandy, gesturing to the box at his feet. "Awards and accolades to stand with the best of them. But our poor lad seems to spend all his time trying to live down the sins of the past." He sighed. "You know, one of the reasons Street had to leave this morning was to deal with that dreadful situation down south. The toxic sludge in the basements. Of course, Barry Tarr's right," he mut-

159

tered, waving his hand in the direction of Rachel's copy of the *Clarion*. "Nobody's seen it on the news. But do you know why? Because as soon as the problem came to light, Street took responsibility, that's why. Darned reporters! There's no scandal involved, so it's not newsworthy." Sandy clenched his fists. "It's not a toxic waste dump, Rachel. It's a few barrels of something, dumped in a field years and years ago. It was never discovered during construction. If it had been, Street would have made certain it was cleaned up. That's what he's doing now. And it won't be on the evening news, because . . . I guess because there aren't big ratings in good news."

"Maybe we need to make them listen. Do you think we could, Sandy?"

"It's not Street's way, Rachel. I used to want him to speak up about it, even tried to convince him to hire a publicist once. But he says that actions speak louder than words, and he won't play their nasty games." Sandy reached across the table and patted her hand. "He's a remarkable man, our Street. It won't always be easy, Rachel. But if you really love him, and I believe you do, you'll trust him."

"I want to. I just need to understand." She sighed wearily, unable to keep her hand from trembling as she set her teacup in its saucer.

"Did Kit let you sleep at all last night?" asked Sandy.

"She was terribly restless, afraid to have the lights off at first. By about five, though, she'd calmed down. I held her hand, and she slept till they rang the breakfast bell."

"She slept . . . not you?"

"With everything running around in my mind, I could hardly lie still, let alone sleep."

"All right. Some rest's the thing then. I've got some calls to make, and cleanup to do. But after that's done, I want to visit our little Kit. Take yourself upstairs, young lady, no arguments now. The bed's all made up in the guest room. Turn right at the top of the stairs."

160

She was about to refuse when Sandy shook his head and pointed toward the hall. There was no point in arguing. "You'll wake me when it's time to go?"

"I promise. Now march! You need to sleep, *cara*. I'm the one who'll have to face Street if I let you get run-down and sick."

Chuckling to herself, and comforted by Sandy's obvious affection for her, Rachel followed his pointing finger and slowly climbed the stairs. Turn right at the top, he'd said, and she did, but stopped to look over her shoulder at the open door to the left. Street's room. She remembered standing in that room, not long ago, the intense awareness of him, almost as if he were there. Street's room.

It was just as she remembered, warm and welcoming, with a hint of sandalwood in the air. Sinking wearily onto his bed, she tried to imagine him by her side instead of hundreds of miles away.

He kept a cluster of photos on the bedside table, many of Kit alone, a few of Sandy, even one of herself, laughing, caught off guard on their day at the quarry. That happy time seemed so long ago. Much, much longer than the two days she knew it to be.

"I love you," she whispered, resting her head on Street's pillow. "Please come home soon."

"Rachel?"

"Mmmm." She snuggled closer, wrapping her arms around him, and whispering his name through the fog of sleep. "Street . . ."

"Er . . . ahem. Rachel, dear, it's time to wake up." Sandy smiled down at her tiny form, curled around Street's pillow in the big pine bed. As her eyes fluttered open, and the panic of confusion flooded her face, he spoke again. "It's all right, *cara mia*. You're safe in Street's bed. I've brought you some tea and toast, and a little surprise."

"Oh, gosh. I—I'm sorry, Sandy. I just needed to feel

161

close to him for a minute. I didn't intend to fall asleep here, really.''

"That's quite all right. I'm certain Street wouldn't mind a bit.''

Rachel pulled herself up in the bed to stare, wide-eyed, at the tray Sandy placed on her lap. A single white rose, its petals just beginning to curl open, stood in a bud vase beside her teacup. "This can't be the same rose!''

"The very same, my dear. I swear.''

"It's beautiful. Sandy, thank you so much.''

"You're very welcome, my dear.'' He moved to the foot of the bed, perching primly on the edge. "Now, Rachel, eat your toast. It's nearly three, and our little Kit is waiting for us.''

"Three?'' Rachel sputtered the word through a mouthful of toast and jam. "You let me sleep too long, Sandy.''

"Not at all, my dear. Nurse Rina kept our wanderer so busy this morning that she fell sound asleep after lunch, and hasn't moved an inch.''

Rachel sipped her tea and took another nibble of toast. "Oh, Sandy, how are we ever going to keep her safe?''

"Problem solved, I do believe.''

"What? How . . . ?''

"I made some calls while you were asleep, and everything's taken care of. By this time tomorrow, Kit will have a lovely new bracelet on her wrist. I understand it's quite attractive, so I'm sure she'll be happy to wear it.'' Sandy winked conspiratorially. "But there's a lot more to this particular bracelet than meets the eye.''

"Tell me.''

"Well, it has a built-in sensor that will react if Kit wanders beyond the boundaries we program into the monitoring device. It will beep at her, just a gentle reminder that she needs to tell someone what she's up to. Of course, the nursing staff will hear the alert at the same time.''

"What a wonderful idea. Sandy, you really are a miracle worker.''

Chapter Nineteen

Rachel slammed on the brakes, bringing the old Jeep to a screeching halt. There was a brand-new gate, an *enormous* new gate at the entrance to Quarry Road. And, at this particular moment, there was a large and round-bellied man directing some heavy machinery through it. Pushing open the door, she stepped slowly and shakily onto the road. What on earth was going on?

"Excuse me!" she yelled, but her voice was no match for the din of backhoes and graders, roaring and grinding their way along the gravel road. Moving closer, she tried again, louder than before. *"Excuse me!"*

The round-bellied man turned with a grunt of surprise and waddled toward her, arranging his weatherbeaten features into a leathery smile. "What can I do for you, little sweetheart?" he asked, his voice raspy and rough.

"What's going on here? There's not supposed to be any work done at this site."

The man rubbed his hand along the side of his stubbly jaw, looking Rachel up and down as if she were a delectable morsel of food and he hadn't eaten in quite some time.

163

"Well, you see," he said at last, "it's this way. Somebody ordered this job done. Somebody paid for this job to be done. Somebody hired me to *get* this job done. So here I am, me and my boys, doin' what we get paid for."

Rachel caught herself just in time, grabbing the gate with both hands before her knees could buckle under her. "Who ordered the job?" she asked, holding her breath, steeling herself to endure the answer. After what seemed like an eternity, he cleared his throat and leaned close. A little too close for comfort.

"Well now, darlin', I don't suppose I should be sayin' a thing here. So I won't name names. All's I can really tell ya is that somebody big ordered this job. Big, and important, and head of a large corporation. Now, little lady, does that help you at all?" He leaned even closer, and Rachel took a giant step backward.

Somebody big and important? The head of a large corporation? It could only be Street, but . . . why? Just this morning Leon had issued a memo to stop all work. He'd claimed that the order had come directly from Street. Why would he tell Leon to put things on hold, and then move his own men into place?

"Thank you," she said, feeling a strange numbness overtake her as she stalked away from the gate.

"Hey, don't you want to stick around and watch the action? Why, you might even talk me into—" The rest of the man's words were lost in the clatter of muffler as Rachel revved up the Jeep. She couldn't deal with this. Not now. Not with Kit waiting.

"Look, Rachel. Look what Mrs. Woolsey let me wear. Isn't it pretty?" Kit held out her wrist, dangling a bracelet crowded with tiny gold charms under Rachel's nose. "She says I'm not the only one with a 'noisy' bracelet . . . but mine beeps. This one tinkles." She shook her hand to demonstrate.

"Mmm. Very pretty. So, um, Kit . . . has your bracelet been making a *lot* of noise?"

She wrinkled her nose. "It beeped at me this morning . . . then everybody came running. I felt silly." Kit sighed, studying the narrow silver band on her wrist. "It won't come off, y'know. But that's okay. Bobby wants me to wear it. He says he won't worry about me if I do." She sighed again. "I miss him, Rachel. Don't you?"

"I sure do, sweetie." Rachel dropped her arm around Kit's shoulders and stared forlornly out the library window. She missed him, all right. So much that it hurt. Almost as much as her growing list of unanswered questions.

What on earth was he up to? she wondered. He hadn't been very forthcoming when they'd spoken on the phone. The fact that he'd called her every single day since his hasty departure should have been a comfort. But what was the point of his calls? The two of them seemed to fence around each other, getting nowhere fast.

She hadn't helped matters, acting prickly as a porcupine, talking of little more than the weather, her work, and Kit's progress. Street hadn't had much to say for himself, either. He was even deliberately vague about where he was, calling as if only to hear her voice. Then he'd ask her what was wrong, and conversation would plummet downhill from there because she wouldn't tell him. How could she? Barry Tarr's claims, not to mention his documented evidence, had to be discussed face-to-face, in person, no matter how difficult that might be. So she talked of trivia, and he listened dejectedly, and both of them were miserable. And now, with that dreadful new fence, and all that heavy equipment rolling into the quarry . . . what was she supposed to think?

"Rachel, look!" squealed Kit, dropping her book on the floor as she leapt to her feet. "Bucky's here. He's taking me out for dinner, y'know."

Rachel took a deep breath. No problem. She'd just act as if everything was perfectly fine. She could do that. "Hi,

Sandy,'' she said, trying a little too hard to be bright and cheerful.

"How are you, my dear?'' he asked gently, looking deep into her eyes. She hadn't fooled him, not for a minute. A massive hug from Kit nearly rocked him off his feet, saving Rachel from having to answer the question.

"Bucky, I wanna go change before dinner, like Mrs. Woolsey always does. Wait here for me, okay?''

"Fine. You run along. I won't move an inch.'' His answer seemed to please Kit, and she bounced happily off down the hall, her borrowed bracelet tinkling with every step.

Rachel shifted uncomfortably from one foot to the other. She hadn't counted on being left alone with the man. What was she supposed to say? He spoke first.

"Rachel, my dear, whatever is the matter?'' His bright eyes studied her with genuine concern, crumbling her resolve.

"Oh, Sandy . . . *everything's* wrong. Street's not here . . . I don't even know *where* he is. And the quarry project's supposed to be on hold, according to Leon, but I saw bulldozers there today, and a big new gate. And Barry Tarr says . . . well, you know what he says.''

Sandy gently took her hand between both of his. "I wish,'' he began, and then gruffly cleared his throat. "I wish I could tell you everything you want to know, Rachel, but Street relies on me to keep silent about his business dealings, and I'm afraid I just can't . . .'' He sighed. "But look at the facts. You love Street. He loves you. This, I know. Trust him, Rachel. You have to trust each other.''

Rachel swiped impatiently at her tear-filled eyes. "I want to trust him, Sandy, more than anything. It's just . . . I can't see how anything's going to work out right.'' She pulled away, clenching her fists in frustration. "I can't see anything at all. Except for things I don't understand.''

"Why don't you go home, dear, get a good night's sleep.

166

It looks to me as if you've been burning the candle at both ends. Are you eating, sleeping?''

She shook her head and sighed. ''No appetite. And sleep? It just won't come. I've cleaned a lot of cupboards this week, though. And stripped the wax off the hardwood floor in the guest room.''

''Have a little faith, my dear. And do try to take care of yourself.''

''Thanks, Sandy,'' she whispered, suddenly very weary. ''Would you say good-bye to Kit for me? I think maybe you're right about the early night. It might be just what I need.'' She forced a wry chuckle. ''The way I feel right now, I could sleep through the weekend.''

Sandy gave her shoulder a squeeze and then gently pushed her toward the door. ''It will all be over soon, *cara mia*, and all will be well. I'm sure of it.'' He smiled. ''Things always look better in the morning.''

''I hope so,'' she murmured, almost daring to believe it. But that night, as she tossed and turned in her bed, she couldn't imagine that things would ever look better.

Chapter Twenty

"**S**urprise!" Dotty launched herself into the kitchen, twirled across the floor on tiptoes, and perched herself on the edge of the counter beside Rachel. "Well? What do you think of the new me?"

Rachel turned slowly, prepared to be tactfully kind. "Wow!" Dotty's transformation was nothing short of miraculous and, in the shock of the moment, "wow" was the best she could manage. Apparently, "wow" was good enough for Dotty.

"Really? You're not just saying that, are you?"

"Dotty, you look absolutely wonderful. The dress, the makeup . . . and your *hair*. It's perfect."

Dotty touched her chestnut-brown curls. "It's the real me," she confessed with a giggle. "I've been a blond for so long, I'd forgotten what that was."

"Well, I like the real you, Dotty. I'll bet you've had a lot of compliments."

"Huh. You know Leon, he never notices anything. But Roger and Stu both said they like it . . . and Harry—" She gave the door a bump with her hip and waited until it clicked firmly shut. "Harry asked me out for drinks. Can you believe it? Yuck!" She lowered her voice to a whisper. "I almost told him what a creep he is, but I tried to think of what you'd say, instead."

"And?"

"I told him it'd be unprofessional for us to date."

Boosting herself onto the counter again, she examined her fingernails, oblivious to the blush that colored Rachel's cheeks. Unprofessional? If she only knew. . . .

"Of course," Dotty continued, "the real question is, will Danny like it? What do you think?" She looked up in time to see Rachel choke back a sob. "My gosh, what on earth's the matter?"

"N-nothing, Dotty. I'm fine. Just tired, I guess. This last week's been a rough one."

"I'll say. Listen, Rachel, you'll probably tell me it's none of my business—and I guess that'd be right—but the whole town's talking about it. Why are you trying so hard to keep it a secret?"

"The whole town's talking about what?"

"Aw, c'mon. Everybody knows you were with Street Wellman when his sister went missing. And before you start denying things, remember, I know you, Rachel. Something changed last weekend. I saw it with my own eyes. You were a different woman when you floated in here on Monday. And since Mr. Wellman left town, well, you've been miserable."

"Dotty—" Denial caught in Rachel's throat. How much was she willing to share with the gossip queen? Of course, Dotty probably thought she knew the story already. Might as well make sure she knew the truth. "I met Kit, his sister, at Riverdale Place. I had no idea who she really was. She'd talk for hours on end about her wonderful brother, Bobby. Made him sound like the perfect man. I . . . we finally met last weekend, and—Dotty, Bobby *is* Street Wellman. You could have knocked me over with a feather."

"It's sooo romantic. Street Wellman. Y'know, Rachel,

169

if I can't have him . . . well, I'm glad it's you. Guess this means I won't have any competition for Danny.''

"You never did. At least, not from me. Guess I'd better get busy on that front, or somebody else might steal the 'new you' away before Danny gets a chance.'' Pasting on her best imitation of a smile, Rachel strode toward the door. ''Better get back to work, Dotty, but just for now, can we keep this between us?''

''Just between us, Rachel. We never even had this conversation.''

The walls were moving. Rachel rubbed her eyes, hard. It was just her imagination. Walls didn't move. She tried to ignore it, tried to work, but couldn't hold her train of thought. The walls moved closer.

"No!" She paced the room, stopping at the window that stubbornly refused to open, and stared out at the fences and backyards of the houses on Pearl Street. Not a soul in sight. Strange that, on such a lovely day, no children played on the grass, no gardeners tended their flower beds . . . had everyone disappeared? A moment of panic threatened before she glanced up at the clock. Five past twelve. They were all having lunch.

She sighed, leaning wearily on the windowsill. In her year and a half at BFOK, the little office had never once felt claustrophobic. Until now. It was the stress of the last few days. She knew that. But knowing didn't make it any easier to cope.

Street had been away for eight endless, insufferable days. And Sandy couldn't, or wouldn't, explain the sudden halting of work at BFOK, or the big new gate on Quarry Road, or the heavy equipment she'd seen disappearing into the quarry. Only Street had the answers, but she just couldn't ask him to deal with her doubts and insecurities over the phone. He had enough to worry about.

Feeling utterly miserable, Rachel squeezed her eyes shut, resting her forehead against the cool glass of the windowpane. Last night she'd told herself that things would be better today. "But things are *not* better," she whispered, tightening her grip on the sill. When she opened her eyes, the room seemed to have shrunk a little more, and suddenly her heart began to pound, echoing in her ears like distant thunder. *Get out!*

She fought her way around furniture that suddenly seemed to crowd the room. She struggled with the doorknob, wrenching open the door and throwing herself into the hallway. Leaning heavily against the wall, she shoved her trembling hands into the pockets of her skirt, closed her eyes, fought to catch her breath. She couldn't let Dotty or one of the boys find her here. Not like this.

As the roar in her ears gradually faded, she heard a familiar voice, raised in laughter.

"No way! We couldn't possibly have met before. I'd definitely remember you."

Oh, no. Not him. Not now. Dotty stopped her before she could hide herself away. "There's Rachel now. Look who's here, Rachel. Danny Minelli. He wants to take you to lunch, lucky girl."

There was nowhere to hide. She forced her feet to carry her down the hall. "Hi, Danny." Her voice sounded weak, trembly. He'd be sure to know something was wrong.

"Hey, lovely lady." He took two of his long-legged strides in her direction and came to an abrupt halt, concern clouding his face. "Rachel? What . . . ?"

She flashed him a warning glance, thanking her stars that he knew her well enough to understand. "Gee, Danny, your timing's good, for a change. I didn't bother to make myself a lunch today and I was just starting to feel hungry."

"What?" He gasped, clutching both hands over his heart and staggering backward a step or two. "You mean you're not going to make some lame excuse to avoid me again?"

"Just give me a minute, will you, Danny? I need to speak to Dotty about something. Why don't I meet you outside?"

171

He nodded, flashing a charming smile in Dotty's direction as he loped out the door. "*Very* nice to meet you."

Dotty sighed. "I really owe you for this one, Rachel. What a hunk! He looks so adorable in those overalls. Don't you just love the way he lets that one strap hang off his shoulder? And the ponytail? And the tan?" She wandered to the window to catch another glimpse of Danny, lounging under a tree in the parking lot. "You're not having second thoughts, I hope?"

"Don't worry, no second thoughts. I've got my strategy all worked out. But, to tell you the truth, I think Danny's already hooked. I'll just give him a little nudge in your direction, okay?"

Dotty giggled. "I'll be ready to catch him when he falls."

"You know, that's not a bad idea."

"What?"

"Are you busy for lunch?"

"Well, no. Just avoiding Harry, I guess."

"So, if you just happened to show up at the Dog & Biscuit, and if we just happened to be there, too . . . and if I had to leave for some very good reason . . . What do you think?"

Dotty checked her watch. "It's twelve-thirty. I take lunch at one. See you there at one-fifteen. And I promise to look surprised."

"Surprised and lonely," coached Rachel, sighing as she opened the door. Her own loneliness had suddenly become a very deep and frightening pit that threatened to swallow her up. *Don't think about it,* she warned herself. *Smile.*

"Let's go, Minelli! I'm starved!" She was in the truck before Danny had even thought to get up from his comfortable spot in the shade.

He eyed her suspiciously as he eased behind the wheel. "All right, Rachel. Drop the perky act. What's wrong?"

"Just drive, okay, Danny? Please?"

"This isn't about that girl Dotty, is it? Because I was

172

just fooling around, you know. I mean, she's pretty and all, but I only have eyes for you, lovely lady.''

''Drive!''

''All right. I admit I might have been trying to make you a bit jealous. But, gee, Rachel, I never thought it'd work.''

''Please, Danny . . .''

He revved the engine and slipped the truck into gear. ''I'm driving. Now what's the matter?''

Uh-oh. She knew that tone of voice. Danny was ready to be sympathetic, to hold her hand, to do more than that, if she'd let him. ''I, um, I just . . . I need someone to talk to, Danny. Someone I can trust.''

''You know you can trust me, Rachel,'' he said, gently taking her hand. ''No matter what. I'll always be here for you.''

The flood of tears that began as he spoke grew to a torrent when he squeezed her hand. Danny wheeled the truck off Main Street, into the far corner of the lot behind the Dog & Biscuit. Parked in a patch of shade beneath an old chestnut tree, well away from prying eyes, he pulled Rachel into his arms.

''I—I'm sorry,'' she murmured at last, pulling away, accepting a tissue to swipe at the last trickle of tears. ''I can't believe I did that, Danny. Falling apart like that, it . . . it's not like me.''

''You must have needed it.'' Danny spoke gently, as if afraid to cause her any more pain. ''Tell me about it, Rachel. Please?''

She twisted the tissue in her hands, watching it tighten into a knot, and felt that same knot tighten in the pit of her stomach. ''You won't like what I have to say.''

''Don't worry about that,'' he replied, inching closer, ready to wrap his arms around her again.

''No!''

Danny jumped, drew back, folded his arms across the steering wheel. ''Sorry,'' he muttered, staring into the dis-

173

tance. "I don't know what you want me to do, Rachel. How can I help you?"

"Oh, Danny, I'm sorry. I—I haven't been fair to you. I'm involved with someone else. That's why I've been avoiding you. I feel so . . . so mean."

Danny rested his head on his arms and forced a little grin. "There's not a mean bone in your body, Rachel. So who's the lucky guy?"

"At first, I thought I was wrong to feel the way I do about him. I thought it was impossible—best forgotten. Then you asked me out, and you were so sweet . . . it made me think about how long we've known each other, what a good friend you are. It just seemed right, somehow, that we should get together. We have so much in common, and he . . . he seemed so . . . strange."

"Who?"

"I got to know him, Danny. He makes me feel . . . I didn't think I'd ever feel that way again." She swallowed the lump in her throat and took a deep breath. "Street Wellman," she whispered. "It's Street Wellman."

Danny blinked, then nodded, as if her confession wasn't much of a surprise at all.

"You knew?"

"I . . . suspected."

Rachel turned in the seat to face him. "Why?"

He shrugged. "The man was too generous, in the first place. Sending the whole crew over to fix your gardens. But your reaction to it was . . . well, unusual. And then Wellman practically raked me over the coals, wanted a word-for-word replay of what you had to say about it. And that Mr. Buchanan, now, he has a way of making you say things . . ." Danny shook his head. "He brought me a glass of iced tea one day, and got me talking about you. It dawned on me afterward that it was a lot more than just idle curiosity."

He stared out the window for a long moment. "I've heard the rumors, too, Rachel. Since the story about his sister hit the paper last week, well, everybody's been talking about it. The things they say about Wellman, though. I don't know. I just don't buy it. He seems like a decent sort to me.''

Rachel smiled. ''Oh, Danny. Thank you. You don't know how much that means to me. It's been a rough week. I feel like I'm living in a fishbowl.''

Danny bristled. ''Who's been bothering you?''

''Nobody, really. Just whispers and sideways looks. The good people of Riverdale are much too polite to come right out and say anything. They'd rather just gossip, and make up stories.''

''Well, I'm not listening. Or talking. And like I said before, I'll always be here for you. Wellman had better watch his step or he'll answer to me.''

''Let's go in,'' said Rachel, giving his arm a squeeze. ''I'm all cried out, I promise. And I have something else to tell you.''

''There's more?''

''No. Something else.'' Her smile came easily this time, and felt natural, thanks to Danny. By trusting her judgment, giving Street the benefit of the doubt, he'd lifted some of the burden from her shoulders. ''I'm parched!'' she said. ''You'll just have to wait to hear the rest. At least until I've had a few big gulps of something cold and wet.''

The interior of Riverdale's Dog & Biscuit was cool, dark, and welcoming—all polished wood and leaded glass, lit with antique Tiffany lamps. ''I love this place, don't you?'' she asked. ''There's something about it, almost like coming home.''

''Remember when we all came here after graduation, Rachel? I had to follow you around all night, begging like a puppy, before you'd dance with me. Things haven't changed much in all these years, have they?''

''Aw, gee, Danny . . .''

''I'm sorry. That wasn't fair. I guess I've always known

175

we'd never be more than friends, but''—he grinned a crooked grin—''can't blame a guy for trying.''

The momentary sadness she'd seen in his eyes flickered out of existence as the waiter delivered their drinks, a cold draft for Danny and a tall glass of iced tea for her.

''Okay,'' said Danny, as Rachel took her second, healthy swallow of tea, ''you're quenched. What gives?''

''Oh, nothing much, really. Apparently, you're not the least bit interested in her.'' She sipped at the tea again. ''Too bad. She's certainly anxious to get together with you . . .''

Danny sat up a little straighter.

''Mmmm. This tea is really good. Not as good as Sandy Buchanan's, of course, but—''

''Rachel!''

She laughed. ''It's Dotty, the 'really pretty' lady you were flirting with a little while ago.'' She paused a moment, letting that information sink in. When the gleam began in Danny's eyes, and a smile played at the corners of his mouth, she continued. ''So? What do you think? Shall I give her your number?''

''Oh, Rachel, that little lady's already got my number. Um . . . er . . . oh! You mean my phone number.''

''Very funny, Danny.''

Shifting suddenly in his seat, Danny stared over her shoulder toward the door. ''And speak of the devil . . . Hey, you two set me up.''

''What do you mean?'' asked Rachel, feigning innocence as she glanced over her shoulder. ''Dotty!'' She waved, beckoning her to join them. ''Coincidence, Danny . . . I swear.''

''Uh-huh. I might have believed you if those big, blue eyes of yours weren't all twinkly. Now cut that out. How can I concentrate on her, with you sitting there being all beautiful?''

Rachel grinned, first at Danny, and then at Dotty who stood smiling sweetly beside their table. ''What a nice surprise, Dotty. I was just apologizing to Danny. I'm about to stand him up again. Would you mind, terribly, keeping him company for me? I forgot about a drawing I promised to finish for Leon. Mustn't keep the boss waiting, right?''

"I wouldn't mind a bit, Rachel. Not one bit." Dotty took her place at the table, laced her fingers together under her chin, and sighed happily.

"I'll just walk back," said Rachel, "maybe pick up a sandwich on the way." No one seemed to notice she was still there. "Okay. Well, I guess I'm the invisible woman all of a sudden." Smiling to herself, she left the two beaming happily at each other. A match well made, she thought. Sandy would approve.

Chapter Twenty-one

The rhythmic swish-squeak of Rachel's porch swing had an almost hypnotic effect on Street. Having settled himself comfortably in the center of the old green-and-white-striped canvas cushion, he folded his arms across his chest and stared lazily up at the gathering clouds. His long legs, stretched halfway across the porch and crossed at the ankles, moved ever so slightly, just enough to keep the swing in motion.

It was good to relax. There hadn't been a single minute of relaxation in the last eight days. No time to unwind. No time to sort things out with Rachel. But that was about to change.

It was good to be home, too, he thought, and chuckled at how easily Riverdale had become just that. R.A.T.S., reporters, and gossips notwithstanding, the old saying was proving to be very true indeed. Home was where the heart is. And his heart was right here, with Rachel.

Street sighed contentedly, banishing the last remnants of big-city tension that had followed him back "from away." He smiled. Sandy had coined that phrase to describe Riverdale's attitude toward outsiders. If you weren't from here, you were "from away." Could be from the next town, or from the moon, it didn't matter. You were a stranger, and not to be trusted. He smiled again. For the Wellmans and Sandy Buchanan, that, too, was about to change.

He glanced at his watch, then off toward the laneway. Where was she? He hated to think of how hard the last week must have been on Rachel. They'd talked by phone every day, about Kit, about the weather, but not about the really important things. Not about the feelings they shared or the million questions that stood between them, needing answers. She'd tried so hard to keep the fear and anger out of her voice, and she'd almost succeeded. Almost. He closed his eyes. "Believe in me, Rachel," he whispered. "Be strong just a little while longer. . . ."

"It'll rain tonight, Rachel. You mark my words." Mr. Parsons studied the clouds and pronounced his forecast with the confidence of a man who'd spent many years reading the sky. "It's a changeable day. Yessiree! I can feel it in my bones!"

Rachel had taken refuge on a broad, flat rock in the midst of the rhododendron bed at Riverdale Place, hoping to steal a few minutes alone for a little peaceful meditation. She peered out at the smiling, white-haired gentleman from behind the waxy green leaves of the shrubbery and did her best to return his smile. "Well," she said pensively, "I, for one, am definitely ready for a change, Mr. Parsons."

He moseyed on up the path, grinning to himself as if he knew a wonderful secret that he'd really love to share with her. "Oh, there's change in the wind, all right." He chuckled. "Just you wait and see. But don't be hiding yourself away in the greenery. That change you're so anxious for might not be able to find you. Take yourself home now, young lady, before it rains."

Rachel shook her head. What on earth was he talking about? she wondered, gazing thoughtfully up at the sky.

179

Far in the distance, a rumble of thunder rolled through the gathering clouds and she shivered in the suddenly cool air. Maybe home was a good idea after all, she thought, brushing the dry leaves and pine litter from her skirt as she stood.

She was feeling terribly lonely again, uncharacteristically sorry for herself. It had been a long and perplexing afternoon, and she couldn't help rehashing the strange series of events as she made her way across the lawns to her car.

Unwilling to tempt the demons of claustrophobia twice in one day, she'd taken her books and plans to BFOK's bright and airy boardroom after lunch, indulging herself in the sheer luxury of space. Leon had found her there, poring over texts and pictures of Victorian-era gardens, and dashing off quick sketches of her thoughts for the museum project.

"Well, there you are," he'd said, blustering through the doorway mid-afternoon. "I thought maybe you'd gone home early . . . *again*." She'd felt it necessary to apologize then, despite her near-perfect attendance record. That's why he'd made such a point of it, she supposed. Her recent absences were definitely not the norm. And so she'd told him how sorry she was for calling in sick last Tuesday, when rumors were flying thick and fast about what she'd been up to with Street Wellman and his sister the night before, and for her early departures more than once in the last few days. She'd made no excuses, just offered her apology, and Leon's reaction had her baffled.

"Perfectly understandable, Rachel," he'd said. "You've been . . . er, that is . . . we've all been, uh, I mean . . . don't give it another thought. I—I'm sure things will be back to normal soon." Then Leon had said the most amazing thing. "You, uh, you look tired, Rachel. Go home and get some rest." He'd cleared his throat, gruffly mumbled something about expecting a phone call, and made a self-conscious exit, leaving her to wonder what on earth had gotten into the man. For the first time in days, she wasn't the least bit tired, and she didn't want to go home.

180

At four o'clock, she'd packed it in for the day, looking forward to unwinding with Kit over a rousing game of Go Fish at Riverdale Place. But Kit was nowhere to be found.

Rina was quick to put her momentary panic to rest. "Mr. Buchanan came by a bit earlier, Rachel, and took Kit out for a drive. Apparently he had to go over to Fairbrook to pick up some things he left at the spa last week. He thought she'd enjoy the trip."

Rachel had started to ask if there wasn't something else she could do to help out, but it seemed that Rina was much too busy to spend another minute chatting and she'd rushed off down the hall. "Kit won't be back till bedtime, Rachel," she'd called over her shoulder. "So why don't you just go home early? Relax for a change."

Rachel didn't want to go home early. She wanted to be busy. She wanted to talk to someone . . . anyone. About anything. Anything to get her mind off Street and the million questions that haunted her every waking moment.

She'd found Mrs. Woolsey in the social room, sharing the couch with the soap-opera set. "Mindless drivel!" That was Mrs. Woolsey's oft-repeated opinion of the afternoon soaps so popular with many of Riverdale's residents. But today, it seemed, she was totally engrossed. "Not now," she'd muttered impatiently, when Rachel attempted to strike up a conversation. "Lola's just about to discover her evil twin in the attic." When a commercial temporarily interrupted the action on the screen, Mrs. Woolsey had turned with a smile and patted her on the arm. "Go home, girl," she'd ordered. "You've been working much too hard. Go home."

It was then that Rachel had decided to take a stroll around the grounds. A few minutes of peace and quiet, a bit of thoughtful meditation, well away from reminders of Street and the quarry. The place, as usual in the late afternoon, was completely deserted, except for dear old Mr. Parsons. And he'd somehow managed to stumble across her hiding place in the rhodos, almost as if he'd been searching for her.

As Rachel climbed into the front seat of the Jeep, she was struck by the rather surprising thought that no fewer than four people had suggested she go home over the course of the last two hours. Wrenching the rearview mirror out of alignment, she stared curiously at her own reflection. She did look a bit tired, but not that bad.

She sighed. Go home? To do what? Clean another cupboard, maybe? Scrub the kitchen floor? Or just sit by the phone, waiting for his call. She glanced up as she backed the car out of her parking spot. There, at the front door, stood Mrs. Woolsey and Mr. Parsons, arm-in-arm and smiling happily in her direction. She waved as she drove away, and the two waved back in unison. Rachel could have sworn she saw Mrs. Woolsey mouth the words ''Go home.''

A clatter of old muffler announced Rachel's arrival as she turned off the highway at The Willows. Leaping to his feet, Street vaulted over the porch railing and hit the ground running, impatient to see her face, to hold her in his arms again. Impatient to make things right. He was still running when Rachel rounded the last bend, leaving the leafy shade of the laneway behind her. The Jeep lurched to a stop as she threw wide the door and raced across the yard to meet him.

''Oh, Rachel.'' He sighed as they fell into each other's arms. ''I've missed you so much!'' Street buried his face in her hair, holding her tight, drinking in the sight, and touch, and scent of her, as if to slake a terrible thirst. He heard her muffled sob, felt her tears dampen his shirt, and he knew. The separation, the doubts and unanswered questions, were more than she could bear. Her pain cut like a knife. Tenderly cupping Rachel's face in his hands, he tipped her head upward and tried to kiss away the tears. He brushed the curls from her face, dried her cheeks with loving fingers, and drew her close again, sheltering her in his arms. "I'm so sorry, my love. I know how terribly hard this has been for you. I'm sorry."

Rachel clung to him, hiding her face in the folds of his shirt. "Street? The quarry! I—I saw bulldozers, and . . . and heavy equipment. Street, you promised! I don't understand. Oh, Street, what . . . what's going on? What have you done?"

"I can't tell you, Rachel," he began, and felt an instant tension grip her body. She tried to push away, gazing up at him, with eyes so full of anguish and fear, he was afraid for a moment that her love for him was lost.

"I have to show you, my love. Not tell you. Trust me, Rachel . . . please." Begging her with every fiber of his being to believe in him, for just a little while longer, Street took her by the hand and pulled her back to the Jeep. "I'll drive," he said gently, and guided her into the passenger seat.

Rachel sat, quietly apprehensive, as Street drove out onto the highway and steered the old car toward the quarry. She let him hold her hand, gently intertwining her fingers with his, but could not bring herself to look at him. Staring helplessly out the window into the distance, she could feel his eyes on her and longed to respond, but she longed for the truth, too. And the truth would have to come first.

Street finally broke the silence. "No more secrets, Rachel. From this moment on, I promise."

Rachel forced her eyes away from the horizon and turned, slowly, to face him. She didn't need to speak. Her eyes said it all. He was going to have to prove it. After all, wasn't he the one who so often said that actions speak louder than words?

The shiny new steel gate on Quarry Road blocked their way, and Street stopped, just inches from its brightly painted bars. Mustard yellow and slate gray. Hideous colors.

"It's temporary," said Street.

He shifted slightly in his seat and then turned to face her as an eerie silence settled around them. Not even a twitter of birdsong in the darkening sky. *The calm before the storm,* thought Rachel grimly.

"It's a magical place, your quarry," whispered Street.

"Not mine. You've made it your quarry, Street."

Something close to anger, or maybe frustration, flashed briefly in his gray eyes as he shook his head. "Look at this place, Rachel. How can this belong to any one person?"

He didn't wait for her reply. "It can't. It shouldn't." He took a deep breath and smiled. "Riverdale wants jobs, and a new beginning. So do I. We'll have our marina, Rachel, but not in the quarry. Sandy's found the perfect location, across the river, just west of town. We'll scale it down a bit, make it something Riverdale can really be proud of. And the quarry—our quarry—it's safe, Rachel. The turtles, the orchids, the osprey, they'll always have a home here. I've made certain of that."

"How?"

Street's eyes sparkled. "I've deeded the lake, and the plant site, to the people of Riverdale. On the condition that it be protected, and kept just as it is now—with one addition."

"Street, you did this for Riverdale? For me?"

He smiled and nodded, lightly running his fingers across her cheek and into her hair. "For us. But you haven't asked about the 'one addition.' Not curious?"

"What? What is it?"

"A community center. The Catherine Laurence Center."

"Oh, Street! Named for Kit?"

He nodded. "For Kit . . . and our mother. The old plant site would be an ideal location, don't you think? It'll be a place for folks to get together, with dressing rooms for the beach, and space for the scuba club and the birders. I asked Leon to put Harry Foxworth to work on a design for the building. The site, of course, is up to you."

184

"But . . . what about the machines I saw? If they're already working . . ."

"That's what I want to show you." Street leapt from the car, unlocked the big gate, and swung it out of their way. "Close your eyes," he ordered, sliding back behind the wheel, "and hold on tight."

Rachel squeezed her eyes shut and gripped the dashboard, white-knuckled, as the Jeep suddenly veered right, and began to climb. "Street? What's going on? Where . . . ?" One eye popped open—she simply couldn't help herself— then both flew wide in amazement. The dozers she'd seen had cut a narrow path up the side of the hill, leading into the beech and pine forest on the ridge above Kit's "magic rock."

"You're peeking," Street scolded, and laughed at the astonished expression on her face as he parked in a clearing on the height of land overlooking Quarry Lake.

"This is where the lodge was going to be, b-but that's too small to be the lodge," she stammered, staring at the shell of a building, nestled among the red pines at the edge of the clearing. Bare bones, that's all it was, just a frame, with roughed-in roof and plank floor. "What . . . ?" She was suddenly speechless.

Street climbed out of the Jeep, pulling her across the seat and into his arms. "It's not the lodge, my love. It's a house. A home." Bending to kiss her lightly on the lips he whispered, "Our home. If you'll say yes."

Rachel's eyes shone as she gazed up into the face of the man she loved, with the certain knowledge that he loved her, too. More than anything.

"Marry me, Rachel . . . *say yes*."

"Yes," she whispered. *"Yes!"*

As the first drops of rain began to fall, Street swept her into his arms and carried her across the threshold, or at least across what would someday be the threshold, of their home. "I've been wondering," he said between kisses, "about a name for this place. Maybe . . . The Pines. What do you think?"

"I think I love you, Street Wellman." She laughed, suddenly remembering two unexpected visitors at The Willows. "And I think I'm about to make Ted and Amy Watson very, very happy." She gleefully shared their story with Street. "Now put me down. I want to look at our house. What's that?"

Street deposited her gently on the floor and followed her to the far corner of the room. "Sandy's been here." He chuckled.

"He did this for us?" Rachel dropped to her knees, pulling Street to the floor beside her. A belated dinner for two. Sandy had remembered every detail—linen tablecloth, three candles, even a single white rose on her plate. As Street lit the candles, Rachel lifted the lid of the picnic hamper and laughed. "You'll never believe this." She chuckled. "Cheese-and-pickle sandwiches, Sandy Buchanan-style. Look at this, Street, homemade bread, little slivers of Sandy's special icicle pickles, and—" She tasted the cheese. "Sharp cheddar, my favorite."

A flash of light and a sudden clap of thunder sent her shivering into Street's arms and they turned together to watch the sky. Forks of lightning split the heavens above Quarry Lake and the rain rolled toward them in seemingly endless sheets. Frightened by the fury and sheer power of the storm, Rachel snuggled deeper into the safety of Street's embrace.

"Don't worry, love," he murmured, nuzzling her ear. "The quarry's magical, remember? And, just like our love, it's rock solid."